Wyandotte Bound

SPEAKING VOLUMES, LLC
NAPLES, FLORIDA
2019

Wyandotte Bound

ISBN 978-1-64540-120-9

Wyandotte Bound

GEORGE T. ARNOLD

Dedication

Every Saturday afternoon when we were growing up, the Arnold kids and scores of other children packed the Palace Theater in Beckley, West Virginia, for five or six hours of B-grade western movies, one or two cartoons, and a serial that week after week featured Clyde Beatty fending off lions with a chair and a whip.

For twenty-five cents, parents enjoyed a restful break in their weekend, and they could feel guiltless because there was no other place their youngsters would rather be. That lone quarter, by the way, included fifteen cents for a ticket, and a nickel each for a bag of popcorn soaked in butter or a candy bar much bigger than they are today, plus a soft drink. Those afternoons were almost heaven in West Virginia and in countless other similar movie houses in towns and in cities all over the United States.

Movies ran continuously back then, and we paid no attention to whether we arrived at the beginning, the middle, or the end because we always watched everything twice.

Our favorites were Roy Rogers and Gene Autry, who, in my view, were the biggest stars of the era. Our other heroes included The Lone Ranger, Lash LaRue, Whip Wilson, the Durango Kid, Johnny Mack Brown, Tex Ritter, The Cisco Kid, Hopalong Cassidy, Allen Rocky Lane, Rex Allen, and Red Rider and Little Beaver. Not to overlook some of their most famous sidekicks: Gabby Hayes, Andy Devine, Pat Buttram, Smiley Burnette, Walter Brennan, Tonto (Jay Silverheels), Fuzzy Knight, and Dale Evans.

We laughed through cartoons like Woody Woodpecker, Bugs Bunny, Tom and Jerry, Mighty Mouse, Casper the Friendly Ghost, and so many others. And the audience went nuts whenever The Three Stooges appeared on the screen.

Few if any of us ever lost our love of stories of the Old West, even after we reluctantly accepted the fact that we were not going to grow up to be cowboys or cowgirls. We graduated to the Grade-A westerns featuring great actors like John Wayne, Jimmy Stewart, Gregory Peck, Alan Ladd, Randolph Scott, Glenn Ford, and Gary Cooper.

Decades later we revisit those days through reruns of classics such as "Duel in the Sun," "The Searchers," "The Man Who Shot Liberty Valance," "The Fastest Gun Alive," "High Noon," "Fort Apache," "Hondo," "Winchester 73," "The Magnificent Seven," "Stagecoach," "Shane," "The Good, the Bad and the Ugly," "Gunfight at the OK Corral" (1957 version), "One-Eyed Jacks," and the lesser known but excellent "Cimarron."

We loved those stories then, and we love them still. For me and my "sidekicks" that wonderful world of westerns started at the Palace. So I dedicate this book to my boyhood friends and to that little theater with its popcorn smell, noisy projection booth, and sticky floors.

Part 1

The Transformation of the Reluctant Gunfighter

When that dreaded day comes, as it surely will, J.D. Rohr knows that only God Himself can save him from his inevitable rendezvous with violent death.

Chapter One

Drifting

J.D. Rohr hadn't been in that squalid cow town saloon any longer than it had taken its grimy bartender to pour him a drink of cheap whiskey when trouble began. Familiar trouble.

He was bone-tired after spending five days in the saddle, destined for Wyandotte, about three hundred miles farther northwest, up Nevada way. All he wanted was a hot meal, a clean bed, and a few supplies when he rode into Concho, Arizona, home of The Cattle Baron, the pretentiously named bar and hash house in which he now stood, facing yet another pathetic nobody eager to risk his life for instant notoriety as a gunfighter.

"You J.D. Rohr?" the stranger demands, in as menacing a tone as he can muster. J.D. sighs, partly out of weariness and more than a little out of annoyance, as he turns slightly to connect the voice to a jittery young man standing wide-legged about eight feet away.

"Yeah," J.D. allows matter of factly, leaving the pressure of the next word to the tall, slightly built wannabe with bad teeth and sallow complexion. J.D. has no clue who this man is, but he knows the type. He has killed five others like him in the two years since he himself outdrew the ironically misnamed Angel Dutch Hendriks, a notorious outlaw feared throughout the southwest.

Unfortunately for J.D., there were witnesses to his fast draw—a dozen or so. And it didn't take long for his legend to build and spread widely. After that the reputation-seekers arrived fast and frequently.

"The name's Colton Skyler," the gunslinger announces too loudly, making sure he is heard by everyone in the room, "and I'm gonna put your ass in your grave."

J.D. sets his drink gently on the bar to free his right hand for a fight he doesn't want but recognizes he can't avoid. The challenger's determination is as baldly obvious as his foolish judgment.

"Don't know you," J.D. replies slowly and deliberately. "But I'll say this just once: If *your sorry ass* ain't out the door before I empty my drink, I will shoot you dead where you stand."

The man in the long oilskin duster blinks noticeably but manages to square his shoulders and push his coattail behind him, revealing a 44-40 Colt revolver stuck loosely in a low-slung holster tied down to his right thigh. That move clears the area around the bar. The cowhands, barmaids, and gamblers have spent more than enough time in saloons to know what's coming.

J.D. takes a slow breath and awaits the inevitable. That glory-coveting fool looks a mite shaken by J.D.'s calm demeanor, but he has brazened himself in too deep to back down. He makes his move and is dead the instant he draws his pistol, J.D.'s bullet stopping the beating of his heart as he slumps backward onto the spit, dirt, and litter covering the filthy floor.

A half hour later, after the sheriff has satisfied himself from eyewitness accounts that the killing is justified, J.D. sits down in a slightly cleaner adjoining room to what he wanted when he entered the saloon less than an hour before—a dinner of strong coffee, a thick steak, and a generous slice of apple pie that isn't half bad.

The sheriff gives J.D. until noon the next day to get out of town. "Not your fault I know, J.D. But you'll just attract more reputation-seekers, and I'll not abide any more killings in my town. So by this time tomorrow, I want J.D. Rohr to be just a bad memory to the folks around here."

Having to leave bothers J.D. not at all, and the killing not much more. He's already gotten most of the guilt, regret, and sick-to-his-guts feelings out of his system after the first two or three yahoos gave him no choice but to pull his Smith & Wesson Schofield revolver. No choice, that is, but to die himself, and at twenty-four he isn't ready for that just yet. So, J.D. eats his meal, rolls himself a smoke, and steps outside into the cooling night air.

The lonely traveler turns reflective as he gazes at the hilly horizon illuminated by a full moon and more stars than he can remember seeing in a long while. He doesn't often let his guard down, but tonight he cannot help thinking about his past. "God, I miss home," he mutters to himself. "Maybe I should've stayed on Dad's ranch after all—much as I hated it."

Back home he at least had loved ones and friends. People he cared about and who cared about him in return. He has no one in these parts, not even an acquaintance, much less a compadre.

"Hell of a way to live," J.D. whispers regrettably.

"No job, no plans, no where in particular to go, and no prospects. By anybody's reckoning, my life's downright sorry," he sighs.

Not at all what J.D. had envisioned when he took the job five years back as deputy sheriff of Big View, Colorado, the only place, up to then, he had ever lived. He hadn't expected the offer from the long-time sheriff, a friend of his father's and a man he had known practically all his life.

But J.D had determined as a youngster on his father's ranch that living in the saddle and breathing dust that smelled like cow manure was not the lifestyle he wanted. Problem was, all he knew was what he didn't want. He'd taken the law job because, at the time, it seemed his only way off the ranch.

For years, he dealt with the boredom of ranch life by honing his handgun skills. That made the transition from cowhand to lawman a little easier. Besides, the work wasn't too bad the first couple of years; it was just demanding on his time. He mostly listened to complaints of the locals about real and imagined wrongs they'd been done, jailed a few drunks on Saturday nights, and saw to it that the whores at Miss Abby's sportin' house stayed out of the respectable part of town.

The killing of Angel Dutch Hendriks, which J.D. just stumbled into while making his rounds one night, changed everything, turning him into a beacon drawing killers to town to try their luck against him. And when it became apparent things weren't going to blow over, in consideration for his family, his friends, and all the other townspeople, he packed up and left.

Knowing scarcely anything about the world beyond Big View, he drifted, taking any kind of honest work he could get—long as it had nothing to do with tending steers. Night clerk at a hotel or two, riding shotgun on a stagecoach line, tending bar—even a stint panning gold up in the Indian Creek region of Colorado. Nothing he found satisfying. Nothing that helped him identify who J.D. Rohr was or might become.

"Hope we find something better in Wyandotte," he whispers to his horse, Patches, as they leave early the next morning. J.D. habitually talks to his black and white paint. Unlike human company, Patches just listens. No interruptions, no back talk, no criticism, no demands. Just a thoroughly dependable companion who walks or runs in whatever direction he is prodded, for as long as needed.

Patches eats whatever J.D. and the environment provide, sleeps in or out of shelter as the situation dictates, and pays no mind to whether his rider ever bathes or changes clothes. "And, unlike a woman," J.D.

observes from his limited experience, "you don't have to be reassured you're loved. Just treatin' you right's all you expect."

J.D. strokes Patches reassuringly up and down his long neck. For days and sometimes weeks at a time, his horse is the only physical contact he has with another living creature.

But J.D. doesn't mind riding alone. Gives him time to think things through. He is uncommonly contemplative for a man with little formal education, although he can read and write well enough, and he knows his numbers.

What sets him apart from men with similar backgrounds are his natural curiosity and skepticism. His interests are wide-ranging and he questions everything, mostly within his own mind, having a singular dislike for those who pontificate publicly. But his skepticism, so far uncontaminated by cynicism, has taught him to think logically and to reach sound conclusions. Most of the time.

Shaking off the maudlin mood that both disgusts and shames him, J.D. steers Patches out of Concho, totally unaware that all of his abilities, talents, and experience—such as they are—will be tested as never before soon after he makes his way to Wyandotte, more than a week hence.

Chapter Two

A Stranded Lady

The trip proves uneventful as J.D. comes within ten miles of his destination. The days have been comfortably warm and the nights dry. He has passed only a few travelers, most of them heading east to find work in the cities after going bust prospecting for gold and silver. He packed enough food and has found an adequate supply of water. No unanticipated dangers. No bad weather. No trouble finding his way.

For the first time since leaving home, J.D. permits himself a smidgen of optimism. And his instincts prove accurate when a brief time later he comes upon a young woman standing beside a broken wheel from her fancy, expensive-looking buggy.

"God Almighty!" J.D. whistles to himself as he approaches her. She is a looker. About twenty years old, near as he can calculate, and wearing fine clothes and hand-tooled leather boots. J.D. speculates that a few generations of her ancestors must have conspired to favor her with their best features. "Yessir," he acknowledges, "Nature has been good to this woman. Real, real good!"

She is about five and a half feet tall with thick dark red hair twisted into a neat braid that falls halfway down her back. Her eyes are the brightest green he's ever seen, and he thoroughly approves of her beautiful face, her narrow waist, and an upper body that strains the top buttons of her white shirt.

The rest of her looks just as good, as far as J.D. can tell. She isn't skinny, by any reckoning, in her tight leather britches, and that suits him just fine. J.D. doesn't take to those pale types who look as if they've never seen the sun or eaten anything that would stick to their ribs. This gal is well cared for, he recognizes, both by herself and by others. She has class—class that he is nowhere near. And he feels it, painfully, right off.

"Got trouble, do you?" J.D. blurts out, realizing too late how self-evident her situation is and how awkward and unimaginative he must sound. Scrambling to recover from his embarrassment, he hurriedly adds, "Can I be of help, ma'am?"

"Maybe," she replies, taking his measure while maintaining her grip on the Winchester rifle she had picked up at his approach. She doesn't know quite what to make of J.D. His appearance seems full of contradictions. He is covered in trail dust. His clothes are cheap, but his boots and his saddle both are well made and carefully chosen. After a good scrubbing, he'd likely prove to be right handsome, she imagines. Tall enough, wide shoulders, plenty of blondish wavy hair in need of a trimming, and a broad, friendly smile that reveals strong, even teeth.

"This man is not some common cowpoke," she concludes.

"If your buggy horse is broke for riding, I can unhitch him and ride bareback while you travel on Patches. I know he looks a little high-spirited, but he'll give you a gentle ride, I assure you. You live close by, I reckon."

"Yes," she confirms, loosening her grip on the rifle. "About three miles or so. I'll gratefully take you up on your offer. My folks are probably starting to worry about me.

"My name's Stephanie, Stephanie Van Shelton," she adds, and offers him her hand.

"Mine's Jesse, Jesse Bodine," he replies, amazed at his quick thinking. He'd determined some time ago to put "J.D. Rohr" on the shelf, so he could make a fresh start in Nevada. He doesn't know if his reputation has traveled this far, but he isn't going to risk it.

He hadn't previously thought out what he was going to call himself, but Jesse Bodine will do right well. Jesse is his real first name and Bodine his mother's maiden name. He never liked Jesse, preferring to go by his initials, but Jesse is familiar enough to him that he can answer to it more naturally than something he just made up.

She is traveling with only a few packages she picked up in town, so "Jesse," as he'll go by for the time being, ties those to his saddle, and they soon are on their way, riding side by side.

"Pretty country," Jesse observes as a way of making conversation, hoping she will pick it up from there.

"Very pretty," she agrees. "My grandparents settled out here decades ago, and they showed foresight. It's good land."

"What's your family's business, if you don't mind my asking?" Jesse inquires.

"Cattle, mining, timber, mostly," she enumerates. "My father and two brothers take care of all that. I've spent most of my time since childhood attending school back East. Been back about a year now and still feel as if I'm settling in. I love it here, but it's not at all like the life I lived the previous eight years."

She rambles on for a time about the contrast between her early years in the West and her teen years on the other side of the country. Then she trains those big gorgeous eyes on Jesse and inquires, "What's your line of work, Jesse, and what brings you to these parts?"

"Oh, a little of this and a little of that," Jesse says evasively. "Because Wyandotte is a growing area, I'm hoping to find some work I'll enjoy doing. If I can, I plan to stay for a while. Been mostly traveling the past two years, and I've had just about enough of it."

"Maybe my folks will know about a job or two," Stephanie offers. "I'll ask for you, and it won't be long because we're getting ready to enter our property."

Jesse sees the entrance as they round the bend. He can't miss it. It is impressive. Two stone columns about fifteen feet tall with large metal letters attached between them proclaiming this to be The Golden Eagle Ranch. Stephanie's expensive clothes and the fancy buggy combine with this huge sign to make clear to Jesse that the Van Shelton family is rich and undoubtedly powerful.

Any question to the contrary is instantly removed about ten minutes later when the house comes into view. Only it isn't a house in any traditional sense; it is indeed a western mansion.

Made of native stone and red cedar logs, it has a rustic elegance, ranging from one to three stories high and spread over a vast amount of land. More windows than he can count provide family and visitors with breathtaking views of hills, forests, and a wide lake fed by a mountain stream.

Jesse, who has never seen the like, cannot suppress the long whistle that escapes his lips.

Chapter Three

The Van Sheltons

Stephanie is right in thinking her parents are anxious about her, for they are waiting at the bottom of the front porch steps when she rides up on a stranger's horse while he is sitting atop a working animal without its buggy.

"Are you all right, dear?" her mother asks, relieved to observe nothing physically wrong with her daughter.

"What happened?" her father wants to know. "And who is this man you're with?"

"I'm just fine," she confirms, speaking calmly. "And this is Jesse Bodine. He came to my aid after a wheel broke on the buggy, and let me assure you he has been a perfect gentleman."

"Well, then, we're in your debt, Mr. Bodine," her father says, reaching up to shake Jesse's hand. "I'm Vincent Van Shelton and this is my wife, Marissa.

"Pleased to meet you both," Jesse replies, smiling pleasantly and trying his best to appear as civilized as possible, given his rough, untidy appearance. He is glad he slipped his pistol and belt into his saddlebags when he and Stephanie passed through the entrance to The Golden Eagle.

"Mr. Bodine, unless you have pressing business elsewhere, we'd be pleased to have you as a dinner and overnight guest," Mrs. Van Shelton offers. "Please say yes. It's the least we can do to show our appreciation."

"Thank you. I accept with pleasure, Mrs. Van Shelton, and, please, call me Jesse."

With the Van Sheltons in the lead, they step through massive double doors and enter the house. It is breathtaking, and quite a contrast to the exterior. Jesse imagines himself in a New York City museum. Beautiful wood and marble everywhere. Enormous crystal chandeliers. Dual staircases leading, goodness, to the heavens perhaps. Heavily framed works of art. Furniture he wouldn't attempt to describe.

Jesse feels so out of place, he is tempted to run to his horse and get away as fast as Patches can move. But he is too intrigued, and, besides, Stephanie has promised to guide him on a "Nickel Tour" after supper. There are sitting rooms, game rooms, smoking rooms, bedrooms, an exercise room, and Lord knows what else to explore.

"We even have a ballroom," Stephanie giggles. "It's true, as odd as it may sound out here in the 'wilderness' of Nevada. My mother loves to dance so much, she insisted my father include it in the building plans." Stephanie says it teasingly, but Jesse does not doubt it is true. He is overwhelmed.

Stephanie gives Jesse the loan of some clothes belonging to her oldest brother, Ruben, who is about Jesse's height but built less robustly. They are a tad tight, but Jesse figures they'll do. Sure beats what he was wearing when he arrived, and at least he is clean, and his hair is brushed. He'll be passable for the dining room.

And what a meal! Maybe the best Jesse has ever eaten. "You could feed a whole dang army from this table," Jesse reasons as he surveys the ham, turkey, beef, salads and side dishes galore, hot breads with fresh butter, a variety of desserts, fine wines and coffee. And, to Jesse's relief, it is all served in an informal setting with simple eating utensils and everyone dressed in everyday clothes. And most of all, the presence of the alluring Stephanie.

Jesse is glad only she and her parents are present. The brothers are returning late this evening, and he is to have breakfast with them in the morning.

Jesse manages to keep them talking about their magnificent house and properties while deflecting questions directed at him. He feels at ease with Mrs. Van Shelton, a slim, dignified, and lovely woman of fifty, and her husband, an extraordinarily handsome, if somewhat over-weight, man two years his wife's senior.

Jesse learns from the fascinating conversation that the Van Sheltons consider themselves first and foremost to be ranchers, but the bulk of their fortune comes from investments made through an old family friend, John William Mackay, richest of those who benefited from a sil-ver bonanza known as the Comstock Lode. At Mr. Mackay's behest, Mr. Van Shelton also became a major partner in the Carson and Tahoe Lumber and Fluming Company, a lucrative business that provides tim-ber for the mines.

As for the tour, it is mostly a blur that hardly registers in Jesse's mind. All he can recall is Stephanie pointing gracefully, concentrating on descriptions and details while he focuses all his attention on her. Jes-sie studies every detail of her beautiful face and tantalizing body and commits each to memory.

He cannot detect a single flaw. She is fresh, young, merry, full of life—shielded against the harshness and hardships that dilute the happi-ness of ordinary folk.

Stephanie surely must know she is extraordinary, Jesse reasons, but he has no doubt she is innocently unaware of just how deeply she trig-gers his instinctive ardor.

Jesse struggles inwardly to control the passion permeating his entire body. And that scares him mightily. Scares this man who has faced down six challengers in one-on-one gunfights. Scares this man who has voluntarily given up the only life he's ever known to keep killers from stalking his hometown and now finds himself baseless, nearly broke, and without prospects.

"You're headed for heartbreak," he cautions himself. "There's no way in this life that Stephanie, or any other woman like her, will ever be yours. Best get on your horse first thing in the morning and run. Ride like hell."

Chapter Four

The Brothers and an Offer

Jesse can hardly believe Ruben and Bram are brothers. Ruben, whose clothes Jesse is still dressed in from the night before, looks every inch an eastern businessman. He is freshly shaved and his hair short and neat. Richly dressed in a gray double-breasted suit, fine white shirt and silk tie, he is wearing lace-up shoes, which also are gray, the first Jesse has ever seen that color.

He and his father obviously are the brains behind the family businesses. Mr. Van Shelton provides a lifetime of on-the-job experience, and Ruben, at twenty-eight, is Harvard educated, sophisticated, well traveled, and confident—if somewhat effeminate in both physique and manner of speech. His light pinkish skin, pale green eyes, and delicate nose and chin combine to give him an appearance that is closer to being pretty than handsome. It is evident Ruben spends none of his time busting broncos.

Bram, on the other hand, could easily be mistaken for Jesse's brother. Shorter than his father and Ruben but more powerfully built, he looks like an ordinary ranch hand. His face is rugged, sunburned to a deep leathery tan from spending his life outdoors. He has eyes so dark they are intimidating, and his nose and a couple of knuckles on each hand bear the unmistakable signs of bones broken either by hard work or saloon fights—or both. His only softening feature is his raven black hair, so curly it grows into ringlets unless he keeps it closely cropped. His rumpled clothes are ordinary, his boots scuffed and unpolished. He has a three-day growth of whiskers and is wearing his sweat-stained cowboy hat at the breakfast table.

To the hired help, Bram, two years Ruben's junior, is known simply as "Boss." He runs everything on the ranch between the buying and the selling of the cattle, which is done by his father and brother. Bram cares nothing about his appearance and doesn't give a hoot about education, fancy clothes, or fine manners. He works hard, demands the same from his crews, and plays hard when he has the time. He also is reputed to have a fondness for whiskey, gambling, and whores.

"Thank God," Jesse mumbles to himself with a measure of relief. "There's at least one member of this family I can identify with."

Jesse's hastily drawn first impressions, however, prove premature and astonishingly inaccurate. Ruben is not at all snobbish and remote, as Jesse had anticipated. He is friendly, solicitous, and seems genuinely interested in getting to know Jesse. He expresses his gratitude for the care Jesse gave Stephanie the previous day.

Bram, it seems, is a first-class asshole.

He treats Jesse like a saddle bum, much to Ruben's embarrassment, asking personal questions and inquiring about how soon Jesse will be off their property. Bram chews with his mouth open, slurps his coffee, and belches freely—all seemingly in defiance of his older brother. It is clear no love is lost between the two.

Jesse tolerates Bram, speaking only when compelled, and then saying as little as possible without appearing rude. Jesse is "itchin' to beat the hell out of that bully." But he holds his tongue and his fists out of deference to Stephanie and the rest of the family—all of whom have treated him kindly and with respect.

Stephanie is waiting for Jesse when he and the brothers leave the breakfast room. "Father wants to talk with you, Jesse," Stephanie smiles. "I told him you're looking for work. He knows everybody, and a recommendation from him carries a lot of weight."

With the faintest of blushes, she adds: "I'm kind of hoping he'll offer you something with us." Jesse is both surprised and flattered, but he has mixed feelings about that possibility. Surely, she couldn't have any romantic notions about him.

"Can't read females for shit," he admits silently.

Stephanie guides him to her father's study where he is greeted with a hearty handshake and pointed toward a chair, just beyond Mr. Van Shelton's handsome cherry desk. Stephanie whispers, "I'll meet you on the front porch when you're finished," and closes the door on her way out.

"Sleep all right?" Mr. Van Shelton inquires in an attempt to put Jesse at ease.

"Fine, sir."

"Breakfast suit you, did it?"

"It was wonderful, Mr. Van Shelton. Much better than I'm accustomed to."

"Good, good," Mr. Van Shelton beams. He'd taken to Jesse right off. Stephanie means the world to him, and he is grateful to Jesse for having treated her right. "Stephanie tells me you're hoping to find work here in Wyandotte and stay put for a while. So, tell me, Jesse, just what kind of work is it you're looking for."

"Well, sir," Jesse starts, "I don't have a profession, just some skills. I was raised on a small cattle ranch, but to be blunt, sir, I hated it. Punching cattle and sleeping out under the stars is not something I particularly enjoy. I can do it. I know all about it, but it's not what I'd pick, given a choice."

"I understand, son," Mr. Van Shelton sympathizes. "Though I have to admit, I'm a little surprised. But I gave all that up, too, when I was a few years older than you and could afford to run the business and hire others to do the day-to-day work. What is it you'd prefer, 'given a choice'?"

"I'm a pretty fair hand at carpentry. Nothing fancy like making furniture or the like. But I can build bunkhouses, barns, small bridges, and repair roofs—things like that. And I can paint well enough to do interior work in houses. Not fine houses like yours, but regular houses, you see. I can repair harness, shoe horses, and fix busted wheels, like on your daughter's buggy. Otherwise, I've done a little bar tending, and I rode shotgun for a time on a stagecoach."

"OK, son, that gives me enough information for what's on my mind. I'm especially interested in that last thing you said, about riding shotgun. I noticed you weren't wearing a gun when you arrived yesterday. Is that your usual habit?"

"No, sir. I wear a gun. Just thought everyone would be more at ease if a stranger you weren't expecting looked as peaceful as possible when he arrived at your door with your daughter."

"So you can use a gun?" Mr. Van Shelton insists, probing a little deeper for a reason he has yet to explain.

"Yes, sir."

"And you're willing to?"

"When I have to," Jesse confirms.

"Jesse, if you'll pardon me for saying so, you haven't been very forthcoming in talking about your past. Anything about you that might concern a potential employer?"

"No, sir. I do have some things I'm moving on from, but I prefer for the time being to keep them to myself. I'm not a wanted man. Haven't broken any laws and don't intend to."

"All right, then, Jessie, let me tell you what I have to offer. I'd like for you to stay on for a time, sort of as an assistant of mine. Mine and Ruben's, that is. You'd be working for the two of us. And let me make clear, you'd not be working for or taking orders from Bram, and I'll make sure he knows it.

"Don't think you two would get along, no offense to you. You see, Bram is used to being the big he-bull on this ranch, and he might see you as a rival, given your youth, your obvious physical attributes, and the fact that I don't see you as a man who would take to being pushed too far.

"If you agree to stay on, we'll start with a few things I'll outline, and then—again no offense—if you prove trustworthy, we'll add more responsibility as time goes on. How does that sound to you, Jesse?"

"I'm interested, sir. But can you give me an idea or two of what you and Ruben might want?"

"Fair enough, son. First, Mrs. Van Shelton is concerned about Stephanie's safety when she's off the ranch. That little episode yesterday with the broken buggy was the last straw for her.

"You see, Jesse, we've allowed Stephanie wide freedom since she's returned from the East because she's a good young woman. She's honest, respectful, and we trust her. But she's too independent. And even though she's determined to look out for herself, her mother and I—and you, Jessie—know she's no match for any low-down man who'd take advantage of a pretty young woman traveling alone.

"So, one of your jobs would be to escort her into town or on visits to neighbors or whatever. Mind you, you wouldn't be either chaperoning or babysitting or anything that demeaning; you'd be protecting her, and I assure you that would be a big relief to me and her mother.

"For another thing, I'd like you to accompany Ruben on his business trips to check on our mining and timber interests. Rough places, all of them. Full of tough men whose behavior isn't always reliable, especially those we've had to discipline or fire."

Leaning forward and lowering his voice to signal confidentiality, Mr. Van Shelton says, "Just between you and me, Ruben's a good man. I have enormous respect for his abilities, but he's no fighter, and I don't want him to be. Jesse, I recognized early on that Ruben was not going to be a man's man. Truth is, I found that disappointing at first. But he won me over with his intelligence and his eagerness to study and to learn.

"He can shoot a rifle, but he doesn't like gun sports, and I don't think he's ever been in a fistfight, much less a gunfight. He's a great business-man and a wonderful, loyal son, husband and father. I love him, and I want him protected, if need be. That'd be another of your responsibilities.

"We can work out the others as time goes on. We have a small house on the property that you can move into, and your wages would be about fifty percent more than what we pay ordinary ranch hands. So, how about it, Jesse? We have a deal?"

"Your offer is very generous, Mr. Van Shelton. I'm grateful and I'm tempted. Can you give me the rest of the day to think it over?"

"Fine, son. We'll talk again after dinner. Meanwhile, I think Stephanie plans to show you around the ranch, if that's all right with you."

"All right with me?" Jesse repeats to himself. "If this good man had even a hint of what I've been dreaming about his daughter, he'd likely shoot me on the spot."

Chapter Five

Settling In

Jesse takes the job.

He has mixed feelings, not sure he has signed on just as an excuse to be near Stephanie or that he actually has the good judgment to recognize a genuine opportunity. The Golden Eagle is a thriving operation. The surroundings are pleasant. The money much more than he'd hoped for. And, just maybe, he can make a good future for himself. Jesse figures he'll play along for a time to see how things pan out.

"If they don't, I can be packed up, on Patches and on the road in less than ten minutes," Jesse assures himself.

Mr. Van Shelton's word is good. He gives Jesse two weeks' pay in advance to make sure he will not have to go without necessaries until payday and treats him with trust and respect.

Mrs. Van Shelton is kindness itself and takes charge personally in seeing that all three rooms of his modest house are clean and well furnished.

For her part, Stephanie is friendly and helpful, but try as he might, Jesse can spot no sign that she wants anything more than a casual relationship with him—all of which he finds puzzling and frustrating.

"Definitely don't know nothin' about women," Jesse laments.

Stephanie doesn't seem to resent Jesse's protective presence around her—and sometimes both her and her mother—on trips to town and to visit friends. They find him to be a man of good judgment. He just naturally senses when to involve himself in their conversations and when to make himself invisible. He'll take any assignment to be around Stephanie. This part of his duties appears to be going smoothly.

Otherwise, Jesse makes himself as useful as he knows how by mending fences, repairing a couple of the outbuildings, and restoring Stephanie's buggy to working order. His first trip with Ruben is coming up in a couple of days, and he's been told they'll be gone about a week on some logging business.

As for Bram, Jesse purposely avoids him. It doesn't take much effort most of the time because Bram prefers to be out on the range with his men and the family's cattle. He hasn't eaten in the mansion since the breakfast he shared with Jesse and Ruben.

Nevertheless, Jesse has a bad feeling about him, and the fact that none of the Van Sheltons speak affectionately about Bram gives Jesse the impression they are glad he chooses to be away most of the time. Nobody questions his ability to do his job; they just don't seem to enjoy his company all that much.

The inevitable run-in comes the morning of Jesse and Ruben's trip to the logging camp near Madison's Creek, a full day's travel away. Jesse is saddling Patches when Bram comes up behind him in the stable.

"Hey, Saddlebum," he sneers. "Just want you to know you ain't fooling me none. I got you all figgered out."

"Meaning?" Jesse retorts.

"Meaning this, Mr. Wise Ass. You got your eye on my sister and my family's money, but it won't do you no good because you'll have to go through me to get either one. You might charm my sister and my mother, and maybe fool my pa and that sissified brother of mine, but I see you for what you are: a ragged-ass drifter who don't know his place. Best you leave while the gittin's good. Understand?"

"Point taken, Bram. I'll hold it in mind," responds Jesse, who outwardly is calm but inside is straining mightily to hold his temper, knowing that if he fights the "Boss" as he sorely wants to, he'll likely be fired, and if he shoots him, he'll surely be hanged.

"See that you do," Bram warns, and as he walks away, he points his trigger finger at Jesse and threatens: "Don't make me have to remind you."

"Well, he said it clear," Jesse understands. "I have a declared enemy. I'll have to be smart if I want to keep my place here and have any chance with Stephanie."

Chapter Six

Mystery Man

"Sorry I had to take yours and Stephanie's escort away for a few days," Mr. Van Shelton says to his wife as they sit having coffee on the breakfast room porch shortly after Ruben and Jesse depart. "I'm going to have one of the other men replace Jesse while he's gone. Just give me a little notice of your plans."

"Vincent, it may seem a little strange, but I'll miss Jesse," Mrs. Van Shelton remarks. "He's such a dear."

"Oh, really, Marissa? That's quite an observation considering his brief time with us. Tell me, what is it about Jesse that impresses you?"

"Well, he's unfailingly dependable and seems genuinely interested in our welfare—even our comfort. He has very good manners, appears always to be in a good mood, and maybe best of all, he has a talent for doing his job without getting into our way."

"Glad to hear all that, my dear. But do you have any concerns? Anything about Jesse that bothers or worries you? In other words, I'm trying to get your overall perception of him. Personally, as much as I like that young man, I have to admit I don't feel I really know him."

"Oh, I suppose my main concern—if you could call it that—is his reticence, being unwilling to reveal anything but superficial details about himself. He's so mysterious. And, Vincent, I'm certainly no expert on this, but he wears that gun of his as if it were an extra appendage he was born with. I have a feeling—no, it's more of a dread—that he not only knows how to use it, but probably has, and not just a time or two."

"I think you're right about that, Marissa. But Jesse has assured me he has broken no laws and is not a wanted man. I believe him. But he has a past he's troubled by, no doubt about that, and I think his past includes more than his share of violence. Perhaps we'll find out in due time. Anything else about him you'd like to tell me?" Mr. Van Shelton asks offhandedly, not expecting to hear anything more of significance.

"Only that he's in love with your daughter."

"In love with my daughter!" Mr. Van Shelton exclaims. "Hell's fire, woman!" he shouts, jolted so hard by the news that he spills hot coffee all over his shirt. "Surely, you don't mean that."

"Oh, yes," Mrs. Van Shelton confirms, chuckling at her husband's reaction and wondering for the umpteenth time in her life how men can be so deaf, dumb, and blind when it comes to things romantic. Not even the smallest business detail can escape Mr. Van Shelton's attention. He knows the number of his cattle down to the newest born calf. Yet he is completely oblivious to the sparks generated when Jesse and Stephanie are in the same room.

Still rattled, Mr. Van Shelton blurts out a string of questions: "How do you know all this? What's your evidence? What's your basis for these audacious conclusions, Marissa?"

"Little things, Vincent. Little things. The way Jesse holds onto her hand just a moment longer than necessary when he helps her into and out of the buggy. The way his face lights up whenever their eyes meet. The way he watches her when we're shopping, and he's pretending to be minding his own business. I tell you, Vincent, he looks at her as if she is the be-all and end-all of his life."

"Oh, my," Mr. Shelton mutters. "Oh, my. Do you think we have a problem, Marissa? Do you know how Stephanie feels? Where's all this heading? I mean– "

"I know precisely what you mean," Mrs. Van Shelton interrupts. "The answer is, I don't know. I'm sure Stephanie is attracted to him, but she hasn't volunteered anything about him. Beyond that, I just don't know."

"But they're so very, very different, Marissa. She's so much better educated. She travels in circles way above him socially and economically. She's used to being wealthy. Heck, she's been spoiled and overly protected all her life, Marissa, and you and I bear most of the responsibility for that. Besides, she has no clue, not the tiniest inkling about how Jesse's world operates. Why, she spends more money on shoes than he earns in a month!"

"I know, dear," Mrs. Van Shelton agrees, a mother's concern spreading across her face. "Everything you say is true. I've thought about all these things myself, and I've concluded that we'd best keep our distance for a while and see what happens. The situation could take care of itself, and there's always a chance we could make things more difficult by interfering.

"For one thing, that young doctor from the prominent Boston family has written Stephanie regularly since she's been home, and he's wanting to come for a visit. I'm going to persuade her to ask him here as soon as he can come. I bet if Stephanie is the least bit receptive, he will propose. Then she'll have a clear choice of what kind of life she wants."

"All right, Marissa. I agree with your strategy. But I really have mixed feelings. She'd fit right into the doctor's lifestyle, but that would mean we'd lose her to his part of the country. We'd be fortunate to see her, and the children they might have, once a year. On the other hand, if she and Jesse have a future together, they'd face a rough adjustment period. But at least we'd have them here, in the big house, or somewhere else nearby on family property. That is, of course, if Jesse's not too stubbornly proud to accept a lifestyle he otherwise couldn't give to Stephanie except by marrying into her family."

"Well see, Vincent."

"Yes, my dear. I hope so. I purely hope so."

Chapter Seven

Unmasked

Jesse and Ruben find they enjoy each other's company as they make their way to Madison's Creek. Despite the enormous differences in their backgrounds, they begin to talk openly as they get to know each other better.

Jesse learns Ruben's wife and children will be returning soon from the East where they've been spending the late spring and summer with her family. She is the former Lillian Tomlinson Wellesley, and her family was among the earliest to settle in New England.

In her lofty social and economic circle, young men and women do not marry so much as they merge with similarly situated families. The Van Sheltons do not possess the pedigree to match that of the Wellesleys, but they have a bigger fortune and that apparently makes up for the difference. Ruben and Lillian have two children, five-year-old Jonathan and three-year-old Esther.

"Lillian and the children spend three months each year with her family," Ruben says, explaining he made her that promise before she agreed to come with him to Nevada, which at the time of their wedding seemed much the same to her as moving to the moon.

He misses her and the children terribly, of course, but he and Lillian have love and a strong marriage, so the annual sacrifice seems worth it. Ruben also loves operating the family businesses with his father. He can get so engrossed in his work he sometimes forgets his wife and children are absent.

As usual, Jesse gives up as little information about himself as he can without being rude. But he pleasantly surprises Ruben when he brings up some historical facts about the settling of Nevada, its entry into the union as the thirty-sixth state in 1864, and its natural resources and topography. As they pass the hours, Ruben is delighted to discover Jesse also is interested in American history and has even read a little classical literature.

"How far did you go in school, Jesse, if that's not too personal a question?" Ruben inquires.

"School ends after the eighth grade in my part of the country," Jesse explains. "Nobody in my family ever went beyond that, and, even if they had wanted to, we didn't have the money to pay room, board, and school costs at some higher-level place."

"Tell you what, Jesse, it seems we have an interest in reading in common, and I have a pretty extensive library at the ranch. I want you to feel free to look it over and borrow anything that has a subject you'd like to know more about."

"That's mighty generous of you, Ruben," Jesse says, pleased to get an opportunity he's never had before. "I'll definitely take you up on your offer."

"I wish you would, but before you think me too generous, Jesse, I must confess my offer is partly self-serving. Frankly, I'd love to have someone in addition to Lillian that I can have meaningful discussions with. Would you like that?"

"Believe I would, Ruben. Yes, indeed, I believe I would."

Arriving at their destination just before dusk, Jesse and Ruben get their horses situated at the livery stable and head to the home of Mrs. Amanda Whittingham, who rents clean rooms and serves fine home-cooked meals.

The town has one hotel, but on his first trip Ruben found it unsuitable. On the recommendation of another member of the logging company board of directors, he introduced himself to Mrs. Whittingham and made a standing reservation with her. She, of course, is delighted to have a man of his quality as a guest. Not only is he a fine gentleman to have staying with her, but he also is a good advertisement for attracting similar boarders.

After a delicious meal of chicken fried golden brown, whipped potatoes with a generous topping of butter, green beans, tomatoes and biscuits—not to overlook the three-layer chocolate cake—Ruben and Jesse retire to their rooms. After breakfast, Ruben will go to the company headquarters to begin three or four days of checking over the books, gathering all the information he can about any business concerns he should know about, and generally satisfying himself that all is as it should be. Jesse is free to spend the days as he wants. They agree to meet each evening at supper.

Over the next three days, Jesse rides Patches into the hills to watch the lumbermen at work cutting trees, hitching them to heavy chains pulled by horses to the flumes that use water to slide the logs to the bottom of the mountain.

Jesse spends several hours watching those two-thousand-pound draft horses, whose tremendous strength and majestic bearing impress him mightily. "History books don't give animals the credit they deserve," Jesse regrets. "I wonder just how much humans could have accomplished without them? No where near as much; that's for sure."

Jesse also visits the sawmills where the logs are cut into timber. It is hard, heavy work, noisy and dirty, covering the men and their surroundings in shavings and chips. Jesse knows immediately this work isn't for him. The only thing he finds attractive about it is the smell of freshly cut wood. And maybe, one other thing: Wood is beautiful in almost any form, but especially when it reaches the final stage in grand houses like the Van Sheltons'.

After supper on the fourth night, Ruben suggests they visit the local saloon. He usually avoids such places, but he feels like having one or two drinks of something stronger than the beverages served by Mrs. Whittingham. Suits Jesse just fine, so off they go.

It is a mistake.

The saloon is dark, dirty, and it stinks. The patrons stink, too. Most have not bathed in memory, and they are loud, vulgar, and rude. Jesse suggests they purchase a bottle of the best the place has to offer and drink it back at Mrs. Whittingham's. Ruben readily agrees.

"Whudsahmatter?" slurs an oversized lumberman wobbling from the excess consumption of whatever rotgut he is drinking. "You and the dude too good to drink with us common laborers?" Jesse hears the words but he can't see where they come from because the man's neglected mustache and beard are so unkempt, they hide his mouth.

"No, partner. We just have enough time to get a bottle and be on our way," Jesse says in a friendly tone, figuring it is better to bend the truth and present an unthreatening front than to antagonize a drunk who is looking for trouble.

"Horse shit," the man scoffs; "I think the tenderfoot there is afraid he'll dirty his suit," he shouts, laughing and pointing to Ruben and prodding his friends to do the same.

"We'll just be on our way, friend," Jesse tries again. "You enjoy the rest of the evening and have a drink on us," Jesse says, putting a coin down on the counter in front of the bartender.

His attempt to placate the man fails. "I don't take kindly to insults," the man threatens, moving a couple of steps forward and looking meaner than hell. "'You 'pologize or I'm going to mess up Mr. Fancy Pants' suit for him."

"Wouldn't try that, if I were you," Jesse warns, his patience at an end. To show he means business, Jesse, who had been facing the bar all the while, turns toward his tormentor, letting him get a good look at the Smith & Wesson.

"So that's the way you want it?" the drunk challenges. "Well, go for it anytime you damn well please."

Just then, another lumberman emerges out of the crowd to intervene if he can. He has been watching Jesse with keen interest. "Let me speak to him, mister, before this goes too far."

"Go ahead," Jesse permits.

The smaller man cups his hand over his friend's ear and whispers something that causes the big man to go saucer-eyed and ghost white. Whatever it is the man said has the desired effect. "Me and my friend will be on our way now, if that's all right?" Jesse nods and the two of them depart quickly out the door and into the darkness.

Ruben and Jesse say little as they make their way back to the boarding house. Ruben has questions, but he figures this is not the proper time to ask them. The significance of what occurred in the saloon, however, has not escaped his attention. Whatever the little man whispered to the drunk scared the hell out of him, and Ruben knows it was not he the man feared. On the trip home, he'd insist on getting an answer to whatever it was about Jesse that put an instant stop to that confrontation.

Jesse, too, is disturbed. Clearly, it was not Jesse Bodine the little man recognized in the bar; it was J.D. Rohr. Jesse will have to deal with that revelation. Everything depends on it.

Chapter Eight

Rustlers

Stephanie is annoyed with herself. Ever since her return from the East, she's allowed herself the luxury of arising whenever she pleases. And that is usually two or three hours after everyone else in the mansion. After all, she has no deadlines for classes, now that she is no longer in school, and it isn't as if she has household chores; the Van Sheltons are rich, very rich, and they have hired help to do all that.

She is arising earlier than is her habit simply because she cannot sleep. That's the way it has been since Jesse Bodine came into her life. And she does not like it, not even a little. She prefers being in complete control of herself.

"Just what is it about this man that affects me so deeply?" she asks herself countless times. "He is nothing, absolutely nothing, like the young men I've known back East. They're all gentlemen, wear fine clothes, and speak perfect English. Every one of them is exceptionally well educated, and they've traveled everywhere. They even know how to do every dance I love."

Of course, they also are all wealthy. More than a few have expressed an interest in her and would propose with her slightest encouragement. She has all the fine qualities these young men appreciate in the other young ladies from aristocratic families, with one fortuitous advantage: Stephanie is blessed with extraordinary beauty.

So why this interest in Jesse? He has no money. He is not well educated, and his prospects are modest. For sure, he is nice and mannerly, but he lacks the refinement and social skills necessary to function in her world.

What is it about him that affects her to the inner core of her feelings? She blushes deeply at the very thought. Perhaps, she really does know why. But young women of her upbringing aren't supposed to have such thoughts. Jesse, she has to admit, is gorgeous. She sees in him the face of an Adonis and the body of a Greek god. There, she has confessed it. Not out loud. Certainly not in front of her mother. But she has faced the unvarnished truth.

The way the very presence of Jessie makes her feel pushes all other considerations out of her mind. To heck with money, refinement, exquisite manners, distinguished families, and all the rest of it. She could marry any number of men who have all that, but, being shockingly honest with herself, Stephanie has to acknowledge that when the lights are extinguished at night, Jesse is the man she wants to be with.

She has shared her feelings with no one, but she suspects her mother knows. Mrs. Van Shelton has caught her continually looking out the windows when the time nears for Jesse and Ruben to return. Stephanie loves Ruben dearly, but she has never before displayed such eagerness for his arrival.

Her mother has complicated matters further by talking her into inviting Dr. Frederick Albert Carlisle to visit, and she does want to see him. She likes him very much. Before Jesse, she was convinced "Freddy" would be the man she eventually would marry.

He truly is a wonderful man with every quality a woman could hope for. But he doesn't dominate her thoughts the way Jesse does, and he certainly doesn't stimulate such passion. Nevertheless, he deserves the chance to make his case, and she owes it to herself to make certain her feelings for Jesse are more than a thrilling infatuation.

From an upstairs window at the front of the mansion, Stephanie sees Jesse and Ruben dismount their horses and turn them over to a stable hand to be cooled down and groomed. But instead of coming directly into the house, the men have their backs turned and their attention focused elsewhere.

There is some sort of commotion, but she can't tell from the window what it is. Curious, Stephanie runs to the stairs, down the steps, and bursts out onto the porch in time to see a rider coming on so hard he raises a visible trail of dust. It is Rufus Meade, by far the smallest of the ranch hands but an outstanding horseman and a valued worker who goes by the uncouth sobriquet of "Shit" Meade, so nicknamed by his colleagues because of his habitual use of the word.

"Rustlers!" Meade yells from twenty-five yards away. "Rustlers, Mr. Ruben," he shouts, so excited he can hardly talk.

"Where, Rufus? Where are these rustlers, and how many of them are there?"

"About seven, maybe eight miles north. I counted six. Could be more. They've cut out several hundred head and are driving them southeast toward Arizona, and maybe on to Mexico would be my best guess."

"OK, Rufus, go get Bram. He'll want to take charge of this."

"But Bram's not here, Mr. Ruben," Rufus responds. "He's in town at . . . I mean, he had to go to town on, uh, some business last night and hasn't got back yet." What Rufus started to say but caught himself in time after noting the presence of Stephanie is that Bram is at the discreetly named Gentlemen's Club, drinking, playing cards, and undoubtedly consorting with a selection of his favorite soiled doves.

"Well, let me talk this over with my father, Rufus. Meantime, alert the hands and get yourself a fresh mount. Town's on the way, and you can pick up Bram there."

Jesse, who has said nothing but has listened intently, asks if he may accompany Ruben to talk with Mr. Van Shelton.

"We'd be grateful to have your input, Jesse." Especially so, Ruben realizes, now that he knows Jesse Bodine is, in fact, J.D. Rohr, the highly skilled gunfighter. He'd be a valuable man in the pursuit of the rustlers, if he and Bram could manage to work together.

On the ride home from Madison's Creek, Jesse had not held back when Ruben insisted on knowing exactly what had transpired in the saloon.

"Ever hear of the notorious J.D. Rohr, Ruben?" Jesse asks as a way of easing into the disclosure.

"I suppose everybody has, Jesse. But what's that got to do with . . . . Oh, wait a minute. Wait a minute! Jesse, you're J.D. Rohr. By golly, you are J.D. Rohr."

"Wish I weren't, Ruben. Wish I was just plain old Jesse Bodine. But I am J.D. Rohr." Letting out a long, slow sigh, Jesse proceeds to explain the necessity of the subterfuge. He tells Ruben in detail about why and how he has chosen his new name. About his attempt to protect the hometown folks in Big View, Colorado, and escape from the reputation-seekers in hopes that, in time, he'd be forgotten. He holds nothing back, and Ruben believes him. Believes every word.

"I can collect my things at The Golden Eagle and be on my way before your good parents and sister will notice my absence," Jesse says regretfully. "Sorry it worked out this way, Ruben. I like it here, and I was starting to feel good about myself again."

"You have no reason not to feel good about yourself, Jesse. You're a victim of circumstances. You didn't set out to kill all those men; you were a lawman. They gave you no choice.

"And as far as leaving is concerned, let me speak with father first. He thinks highly of you, and I know he'll want you to stay unless he believes your presence will attract trouble and endanger the family. Do I have your permission to tell him about you? I promise both of us will keep the information confidential."

"I trust your judgment on this, Ruben, and I'll abide by whatever the two of you decide. No fuss, no argument. My word on it."

With Rufus's news about the rustlers, Ruben and Jesse will have to fill in Mr. Van Shelton fast, both on the revelations about Jesse and the details of the stolen cattle. They find him in his office, smoking a cigar and checking his account books. He is delighted to see them, but word of the rustlers robs him of his momentary happiness. He looks crestfallen when told about Jesse. Given the situation, however, Mr. Van Shelton allows himself only a moment to put it all into context.

"All right, Ruben, and you, too, Jesse. Here's the way it is, and the way it's going to be for the foreseeable future. You're still Jesse Bodine as far as I'm concerned, and you'll remain right here, if you're agreeable. If trouble comes, we'll reassess the situation. Meanwhile, we need to get moving on those rustlers. Let's get outside and talk to the men."

A half dozen ranch hands are waiting at the bottom of the steps, and among them is Bram, just back from town and looking none the worse from the activities of the previous night. Rufus has already filled him in.

"Well, Ruben," Bram taunts, "I know you ain't gonna ride with us, but how 'bout you, Babysitter," he sniggers, aiming his question at Jesse. "You got the balls to join us, or would you rather spend the day having cookies and tea with the ladies?"

"Don't be impertinent, Bram," Ruben says in reproach.

"Don't know what that means, big brother, but I 'spose that's your Harvard talk for shut up."

"I'll say it plain, Bram," Mr. Van Shelton interrupts. "Shut the hell up! We've got a serious situation that demands immediate attention. Besides," Mr. Van Shelton cannot resist adding, "I'm afraid you're badly misjudging Jesse, and that mistake might one day lead to the comeuppance you're so overdue for. Now, let's get on with our business."

Turning to Jesse, Mr. Van Shelton says, "Whether you go or stay is completely up to you, Jesse."

"What would you like me to do, sir?"

"I won't ask you to go," the older man makes clear, "but it will ease my mind some if you do. Bram needs your help, even though he'll not acknowledge it."

"Then I'm in," Jesse decides. "I'll be ready in five minutes."

Chapter Nine

Bram's Comeuppance

With Bram in the lead, Jesse, "Shit" Meade, and a half dozen other cowpokes who'd volunteered their services, catch up in less than half a day with the slow-moving herd and the rustlers, whose actual number is ten. Bram wants to rush right in, but Jesse has a better plan that Bram, amazingly, agrees to because Jesse purposely proposes it modestly so Bram will not lose face.

"We'll wait until they settle the herd down for the night, after they've eaten and most are sleeping. This way the animals are less likely to scatter when we move in, and we'll have only a few men standing guard to deal with."

The battle is brief. Three of the rustlers, all of whom had been asleep, raise their hands in surrender immediately. Three of those standing guard ride the hell away. The remaining four draw their weapons and began firing. Bram and Jesse shoot two each.

"Make certain they're dead," Jesse cautions. He checks his two, and they are indeed dead. Bram glances at the other two. They aren't moving.

"Dead," Bram yells to Jesse, but as he puts his left foot into the stirrup to mount his horse, he yelps in pain as a bullet from one of the "dead" men he was supposed to check cuts into his flesh.

"Shit" Meade responds instantly, shooting the man through his right eye, leaving no doubt this time he is through.

Rushing to Bram, who is writhing in pain on the ground and cursing his luck, Meade demands: "Where ya hit, Boss? Is it serious?"

Bram doesn't reply but everybody gathering around him notices him clutch his left buttock.

Amused, but holding back his laughter until he determines the degree of the injury, Jesse orders Meade and Ross Porter to remove Bram's gun belt and pull down his pants. They do so, in full view of all of the ranch hands, Bram cursing and protesting all the while his bare butt is shining in the moonlight. The wound is bloody and no doubt painful, but he won't die from it.

With that knowledge, "Shit" Meade lets out a howl of ridicule. For years, he has suffered Bram's insults and derisive comments about his size, or rather the lack of it, and now fate had delivered into his hands a delicious opportunity for payback.

"Big Bad Bram got shot in his ah-us, Big Bad Bram got shot in his ah-us," Meade sings at the top of his voice, dancing in a circle around his boss and rubbing it in for all he is worth. The others can't resist joining in.

Thoroughly humiliated, Bram rises above his pain to hurl a string of obscenities at Meade, and with total disregard for the delicacies of language or redundant wording, he adds: "Eat shit and die, you little pygmy runt!"

Bram has gotten the comeuppance his father had predicted, only it comes from his own carelessness instead of from Jesse.

With the cattle recovered and the rustlers subdued or dead, Jesse designates two men to escort the captives to the sheriff's jail in Wyandotte. He'll let the law deal with those who escaped, their arrests being likely if their cohorts give them up in exchange for being spared the rope for rustling.

As for Bram, he is in no condition to sit a saddle, so the men fashion a travois on which he can lie face down and be pulled along by his horse.

It will be a further indignity for Bram, but what the hell, no one deserves it more.

Chapter Ten

Life is Good

Being confined to a bed in the big house is yet another burr under the saddle that Bram will not be sitting on for a good spell. For the first time in his life, Bram is a pain in his own ass. He resents his embarrassing predicament, fussing because he can't sit, complaining at not being able to walk, and grumbling about being bored. He is a lousy patient.

Bram endures, but does not enjoy or find comfort in, visits by the women. He has nothing in common to talk about with his mother, sister, or sister-in-law. Of course, that does not discourage them from dropping by. He can do without the attention of his niece and nephew, too, and he tolerates his brother only for as long as it takes Ruben to bring him up to date on ranch business. The only person he truly welcomes is his father, whom Bram sincerely admires and tries to please.

"You and Jesse and the boys did a fine job in dealing with those rustlers, son," Mr. Van Shelton compliments. "I'm proud of you all and grateful as well."

"Thanks, Pa [Bram refuses to call him father as his 'stuffy' siblings do]," Bram replies, appreciative of the praise from the only person whose opinion matters to him.

"Hope it settles things between you and Jesse, too. I don't think you need any further proof of what he's made of, do you, Bram?"

"Oh, I'll give him his due for his part against the rustlers," Bram allows. "But I still don't trust the sumbitch. He's still after Stephanie and our money, you know."

"I think you're all wet about the money, son. And as far as any interest he might have in your sister is concerned, they're both adults.

What does or does not happen between them is up to them. But I know nothing I can say will convince you otherwise, so let's just leave it at that.

"Anything you need, son? Anything at all?"

"Just let the boys in to visit and keep everybody else out. That's what I'd like. Oh, and you can tell that quack doctor I'm goin' back to the bunkhouse by the weekend, like it or lump it."

Mr. Van Shelton leaves the room shaking his head, and Bram goes back to his solitary sulking.

Jesse makes no attempt to visit. He is as happy to be out of Bram's sight as the "Boss" is to be out of his. This is just one of the small blessings that make life good for Jesse as the weeks pass. He is worried less about being further exposed as J.D. Rohr. Fact is, if he never has to use his revolver again, that will be just fine with him.

The lightning fast draw with the deadly accurate aim that took him years to acquire has done him more harm than good. It forced him from his home and made him a target for a variety of misfits who neither knew him nor had a single complaint against him except for the reputation he has and they wanted.

Happily for Jesse, Ruben has opened a door to education for him, and to the latter's great satisfaction, Jesse is pursuing the opportunity with energy and dedication. Ruben, who loves sharing his considerable knowledge as much as he enjoys acquiring it, proves a gifted teacher. He is patient, encouraging, and seems instinctively to know how much Jesse can handle at one time without being overwhelmed. Ruben plans a course of study on a wide range of liberal arts topics that will, in time, give Jesse the home-study equivalent of a college education. And he has no doubt Jesse is capable of achieving it.

Lillian eventually volunteers her services, too, after she accepts her husband's assurances that Jesse is not some wild westerner from whom she should hide the children. Recognizing Jesse's interest in Stephanie, Lillian figures he will stand a better chance with her if he works on some of the finer skills that come so naturally to Stephanie and her contemporaries.

So she organizes instruction in managing the long line of utensils set before guests at formal dinners, in polishing his abilities at small talk with upper-class strangers, and purging his language of double negatives, in dressing properly for all occasions, and last—but obligatory among the young women—in mastering the art of dancing in a variety of forms. Like Ruben, Lillian is pleased with Jesse's enthusiasm and is literally thrilled to discover his agility and natural sense of rhythm—qualities she is unaware a gunfighter literally could not live without.

In return, Jesse gives a few lessons of his own, guiding Ruben and Lillian's son, Jonathan, in the handling of the pony his grandfather gave him and the lasso made for him by Rufus Meade. Jesse delights their daughter, Esther, by taking her for daily walks with her dog, inexplicable named Winston, and by making her his partner while practicing his newly acquired dance moves. Like virtually all others females throughout the history of the world, Esther loves prancing around a dance floor—and her grandmother has the biggest privately owned one in the state.

Jesse grows fond of the children, and, after a while, warms up to Lillian, who intimidated him at first with her intelligence and her drill sergeant manner of instruction. He has never before encountered a woman like Lillian. She considers herself the equal of any man and doesn't try to sway men with her charm and beauty, as do others of her gender and social class. She says what she thinks directly and without regard to conventionally accepted standards of behavior.

Jesse admires that.

Life is good; so good it gives him an ominous feeling. He soon finds out why: A rival is coming for a visit.

Chapter Eleven

A Rival

Traveling first by train and then by stagecoach, Frederick Albert Carlisle, a doctor of medicine as well as a surgeon, arrives in Wyandotte on the morning of September 14. Stephanie and her father are on hand to welcome him, having arrived in the two-seater surrey equipped with a canopy top that will provide protection, if needed, from the day's threat of rain.

"Freddy," as Stephanie calls him, looks genuinely happy to see them, greeting each with a warm handshake, which, as Mr. Van Shelton observes, is the only sign of affection that passes between the two young people.

"Glad to finally meet you, my boy," Mr. Van Shelton says, assuming a familiarity he hopes will make sure Frederick knows he is most welcome.

"I'm very pleased, sir, to have this opportunity to meet you and the rest of Stephanie's family. I've been looking forward to it ever since she returned home. Tell me, sir, will your sons, as well as your wife, be at the house? I've heard so much about them from Stephanie I feel as if I already know them."

"Marissa and Ruben will be home for certain," Mr. Van Shelton says. "Bram is still out on the range, but we expect him home within a couple of days. Just so you'll know, Frederick, Bram leads a considerably different lifestyle from the rest of us. He's a fine man, but I want you to be prepared for what otherwise might puzzle you about his clothes and his manners."

With the pleasantries out of the way, they begin their ten-mile travel to The Golden Eagle Ranch. While Stephanie engages Frederick in conversation, Mr. Van Shelton takes the opportunity to give his daughter's potential husband a discreet visual going over.

The man looks like a doctor—or at least like most people's stereotypical notion of what a physician should look like: immaculately groomed, conservatively dressed, distinguished, and kindly.

On closer inspection, however, Mr. Van Shelton observes a sturdy physique on a tall frame, possibly six-foot three, a handsome face with a wide, firm jaw, and noteworthy hands. The unusually long fingers could belong to a classical pianist, which Frederick is not, or, as Mr. Van Shelton surmises, they would be quite suitable for performing delicate surgery, which Frederick does routinely.

Furthermore, he finds Frederick to be gregarious and delightfully curious. He will not be impressed by the Van Sheltons' magnificent mansion and its fine furnishings; he has spent a lifetime in such surroundings. Surprisingly, it is the West itself that fascinates him.

As they travel, he asks a string of insightful questions about the land so different from what he is accustomed to back East, the people he encountered on the trains and stagecoaches, and others he met in places where he lodged along the way.

He stuns them by volunteering that he intends to immerse himself in their western culture. "If Bram is willing, I want him to take me to town and outfit me in western wear from head to toe. I want to ride horses with saddles equipped with a 'horn' not found on the eastern models to which I am accustomed. And I fancy myself engaging in all manner of 'cowboy things' like roping and branding calves and sleeping out in the open beside a blazing campfire." Stephanie giggles as she sees her father's eyes roll upward in disbelief.

***

For the next three weeks, all Jesse can do is watch from the periphery as Frederick, with no apparent scheme or ulterior motive, charms virtually everyone on the ranch and in the Van Sheltons' community of friends and public officials. From girls of Esther's age to women of Mrs. Van Shelton's maturity, the females find "Dr. Freddy" dazzling. His wit, his humor, and his incomparable skill at making each of them feel as if his attention centers exclusively on her combine to enhance his considerable popularity.

Not an easy man to win over, Mr. Van Shelton quickly recognizes Frederick is genuine, conceding he is undoubtedly a superior match for Stephanie, although a marriage to him would mean her near permanent absence from his and Mrs. Van Shelton's lives.

Being of the same age and near identical educations, both having graduated from prominent New England schools, Ruben and Frederick have so much in common their friendship is a foregone conclusion.

Even the house workers, as well as the ranch hands, soon shed their reservations and natural distrust of this rich, upper-class easterner. Insisting they call him by his first name, Frederick pops into the kitchen unannounced to prepare gourmet dishes for them as well as for the Van Shelton family to sample. They don't find all of his creations to their liking, but they are flattered by the attention and for being included. Serious about emulating a cowboy lifestyle, Frederick endears himself to Rufus Meade, whom he declines to address as "Shit," and his companions by soliciting their help and advice in his amateurish, but good-natured attempts at trick riding, fancy roping, and good old western cussing.

Surprisingly, Bram—Bram, who will admit to liking only animals, other cowboys, whiskey, cards, and sporting women—thaws a little in

Frederick's presence, going so far as to ride into town with him to outfit the good doctor in cowboy paraphernalia he all but sleeps in for the rest of his visit. Frederick is particularly enamored of the big Stetson hat, large turquoise belt buckle, and high-heeled boots. It is clear that Frederick respects Bram's toughness and his ability to lead other men of similar mettle. As for Bram, he appreciates being appreciated.

Jesse feels totally defeated, and the heck of it is, he, too, likes Frederick, who is ignorant of Jesse's interest in Stephanie. Frederick, Jesse concludes, is simply a fine human being, period. None of this lessens Jesse's love for Stephanie, but he now has no illusions about a life with her. His hopes and dreams are no more realistic than his fantasies. He knows it, as does everyone else—everyone else, that is, except Stephanie herself.

"I'm so proud of Freddy," Stephanie informs her mother as they are getting dressed for dinner. "Everybody on the ranch and in the community is crazy about him. His visit has been such a success."

Mrs. Van Shelton concurs wholeheartedly. "You also realize, don't you, my dear," her mother says, "how commendable it is that Frederick went to school for so long and worked so hard to become a physician and surgeon? After all, with his great wealth and social position, he could have chosen a hedonistic lifestyle, as many young men in his position do."

Stephanie does realize and appreciate all of that, but what she does not tell her mother—indeed, cannot tell her mother—is the maddening truth about her feelings for him. Freddy doesn't make her heart race. And she blames herself.

"What's wrong with me?" she ponders over and again. "Am I really that silly, immature, and superficial?" she wonders. "Is it so wrong for me to want passionate love in my marriage?" Stephanie feels simultaneously blessed and cursed. She prays for wisdom and guidance.

Chapter Twelve

The Soiree

Mrs. Van Shelton's closest friends, and Stephanie's as well, have made quite clear Frederick is not to depart before they are treated to another evening in his presence.

"We will never, ever forgive the two of you," is their common threat—said with the wink of an eye but also meant to be taken most seriously.

So Mrs. Van Shelton is handed a perfect excuse for a soiree, a dinner followed by an evening of dancing. Not that she needs an excuse; she has at least four of them every year, one for each season. With a party, she never lacks for a dancing partner. Besides, she has grown enormously fond of Dr. Freddy and wants to give him a proper send-off.

With Frederick's month-long visit drawing to a close, invitations go out to a small number of fortunate females whose husbands will reluctantly surrender to their wishes, mainly to avoid the icy reception that is certain to follow in the boudoir if they refuse. Dress will be formal, and guests are welcome to spend the night—even their closest neighbors, who in the West live five or more miles away.

Frederick insists on supplementing the usual fare by preparing his favorite dish, one that has never before graced a table in Wyandotte.

"I'm making Fillet of Beef Prince Albert, flavored by a few ounces of white wine and cognac," he announces to his hostess. We'll serve it on wooden skewers, and your guests will love it."

Mrs. Van Shelton is thrilled.

The entire family, including the children, will be on hand—all except Bram, who, to the others' relief, will not even consider attending.

However, Bram, it turns out, will not shun the event entirely. He decided two weeks into Frederick's visit that he'd trade Ruben for the doc any day. So, with the assistance of Rufus Meade, Bram organizes a team of ranch hands to tend to the guests' horses and buggies.

But what to do about Jesse? Would being there be too painful for him, with Stephanie at Frederick's side the entire evening? Would he feel out of place? Awkward at such an event?

"You know how fond I am of Jesse," Mrs. Van Shelton stresses as she seeks counsel from Stephanie, Lillian, and Ruben. "It's not that Vincent and I don't want Jesse to take part; we're just worried for him, not for us."

Stephanie, too, has reservations. "I wouldn't have Jesse's pride hurt for the world," she exclaims. "But I'm afraid his pride would be just as hurt if we don't invite him. Either choice pains me to death."

Ruben and Lillian, however, have their secret knowledge the others know nothing about. So they insist Jesse be asked, and they are the only two not puzzled when Jesse accepts immediately, without persuasion, much less coercion. As for Jesse, he has a surprise or two in mind that might astound everyone except Ruben and Lillian.

Stephanie herself remains conflicted about Frederick and Jesse. She wants Frederick to leave; she wants him to stay. She wants him to propose; she dreads that he might. She dreams of being wrapped in his arms, but it is Jesse's face she sees attached to Freddy's body. "God, if you are going to answer my prayers, you'd better hurry," she pleads, "before I lose my mind."

Regardless of Stephanie's state of mind, The Golden Eagle Ranch is a whirlwind of activity over the next few days, what with so many preparations under way for the big doings. But by the time folks start arriving, the mansion is sparkling from floor to ceiling, a veritable feast has been prepared, an orchestra has been stagecoached in, and all cattle

have been resettled at a sufficient distance to ensure they pose no offense to the guests' olfactory organs. It is indeed a grand show.

Mr. and Mrs. Van Shelton take their positions at opposite ends of
the long, impressively decked out table, with the guest of honor and
Stephanie seated at the center where they will be within comfortable
view. Jesse sits between the children, Jonathan and Esther, whose company he knows he will enjoy most. The eight invited couples are placed
next to or directly across from Frederick and Stephanie. Serving begins,
small talk resumes, and a festive mood settles over the room.

Stephanie watches anxiously as Jesse, splendidly dressed in a suit
Ruben had tailor-made especially for this occasion, begins negotiating
his way through the eating utensils: appetizer fork, salad fork, dinner
fork, dinner knife, dessert fork, and butter knife. She is amazed.

As the meal progresses, Jesse works his way from the outer to the
inner utensils, positioning his fingers perfectly and keeping his arms
tucked in while cutting meat, and never once resting his hands on the
table, much less his elbows. It is as if this were his hundredth formal
dinner instead of his first. Two positions to his left, Lillian also watches
closely, with amusement at the expression on Stephanie's face and pride
in her student. Jesse has learned well.

If Stephanie was surprised at the dinner table, she is absolutely flum-
moxed when the music begins. She and Frederick have the honor of
leading off the first dance, and after they receive the appropriate amount
of attention, the others join in.

Frederick is an accomplished dancer, guiding Stephanie skillfully
and effortlessly around the huge floor. Like her mother, Stephanie loves
dancing, so much she is able to momentarily forget her concerns and
enjoy herself as the orchestra plays Strauss's Blue Danube waltz.

As they dance, she and Frederick nod graciously to the others who
look admiringly at the strikingly beautiful couple. Smiling with

pleasure, Stephanie turns her head to her left and trips clumsily over her own feet, saved from falling only by Frederick's strong grip. She was startled by the sight of Lillian and her partner as they came into view.

Jesse! Her partner is Jesse!! And he is dancing!!! Beautifully!!!! Stephanie all but faints. He may not be as smooth as Frederick, but he is more than holding his own.

She is not the only female in the room whose heart is aflutter. Directives are immediately given to husbands to inform Jesse their wives will never forgive them if they fail to persuade him to take at least one turn with each of them. Jesse, who has never before received this kind of attention from such lovely, intelligent, and accomplished women, complies happily, fulfilling every request.

Except for his good looks, Jesse was barely noticed when the dinner began, but now the esteem in which he is held rises considerably.

Jesse has consumed nothing stronger than wine, but he nevertheless feels joyfully intoxicated, especially when his greatest hope for the evening is fulfilled—a dance with Stephanie. As he takes her hand in his and places his arm lightly around her tiny waist, Jesse feels a slight trembling, one that he prays flows from Stephanie and not from him.

They dance as one body, missing not a step even though each is more focused on the other than on the waltz. Jesse loves the feel of her, her fragrance, her warmth. She, in turn, is excited by Jesse's gracefulness and power, the strength she feels in his hand and arm as he turns her to the left, then to the right and whirls her around and around.

It is the crowning glory of one of the most memorable nights in Jesse's life.

But as euphoric as it is, the moment is not to last. Jesse's worst fears are about to be realized.

Chapter Thirteen

Divine Intervention

Approaching with a grave look on his face, Ruben discreetly takes Jesse aside and whispers that he is to come along to Mr. Van Shelton's office. Saying nothing as they work their way through the guests, they walk into the room where Mr. Van Shelton, Bram, and the town sheriff, Cliff Dalton, sit in silence.

Despite the fine clothes he wears and the heady experience of the enchanting evening, Jesse feels instantaneously reduced to the lowly drifter he was before entering into life with the Van Shelton family. He doesn't have to be told. The cause of the solemn seriousness is evident: J.D. Rohr is back.

The sheriff gives the news to Jesse straight. "The word's out on you, Jesse. Or J.D. Here's how it happened. When you were in town the other day with the Van Shelton women, a little man who stopped in Wyandotte on his way east spotted you. Said he'd seen you in a Madison's Creek saloon with Ruben. Bragged to everybody who would listen about how he saved his friend's life when the fool had gotten drunk enough to dare you to draw your gun.

"Word's gotten around, Jesse. And one of those asshole gunslingers rode in today, and he's looking for you. Says if you aren't in town first thing in the morning, he's coming after you out here at the ranch. And he made a point of saying he don't give a damn if a bystander gets in the way of a bullet."

Dalton's statement is followed by a weighty silence. Mr. Van Shelton and Ruben are thinking desperately, without success, to figure some positive way out of the predicament. Finally, Bram speaks up. "I'll face this with you, Jesse, if you'll allow me the privilege. You cudda drilled my cussed ass any number of times when I was callin' you every insulting name I could come up with." Bram knows he has badly misjudged Jesse and believes he owes him.

"Coming from you, Bram, that means a lot to me. I appreciate it. You, too, Sheriff Dalton, for coming out here to give me a heads up and a chance to get off The Golden Eagle Ranch before I endanger any of the good folks here. But, no, Bram. There's nothing any of you can do.

"I thought for a while I could build a new life here as Jesse Bodine. Wishful thinking on my part. Foolish thinking. I'll be out of here before daybreak, sheriff. And you can give word to the gunslinger I won't be in town. I won't cause you any trouble there. Tell him if he wants me, I'll be headed west."

Sadly, the Van Sheltons know Jesse is right. If he, with or without their help, dispatches this gunslinger, an endless supply of others will show up to take his place. There is no other choice.

Mr. Van Shelton asks the others to keep their seats while he walks Sheriff Dalton to the door. On his return he explains, as head of the family, how he and the other men are to conduct themselves until the party's end. Not a word of what has been said in his office is to be repeated, not even to the other men. Jesse will slip away before dawn.

"It's my duty to tell the women, especially Stephanie, and try to make them understand. I dread it, and, Jesse, we'll miss you more than you'll ever know. Ruben and Bram won't mind if I tell you I feel for you like a father. You don't deserve what's happened to you and how you've had to live as a result.

"But right here and now, with the full support of my sons, I insist— no, make that demand—that you take the money I'm going to give you this moment from my safe. By God, if we can't make possible a life for you on our ranch, we're damned sure going to make certain you're comfortable wherever you go. That's my word on it, and I would be offended by any quibbling on your part, Jesse."

It runs strongly against his grain, but Jesse accepts the big stack of bills. He doesn't want to insult these good men in their last time together.

Fortunately, the party is breaking up as the men return. Mrs. Van Shelton chides them mildly for giving more attention to their cigars and whiskey in her husband's office than to her and the other ladies in the ballroom. The men are grateful for her misinterpretation of the dire event that just occurred.

As the guests not staying overnight make their way to their carriages, family members walk arm-in-arm with their friends, chatting about the wonderful time they've had and trading sincere compliments. Eager to make her contribution, sweet little Esther brings her beloved dog, Winston, and holds him beside the door for all to admire.

Bram and his men watered and fed the guests' horses earlier, and the handsomely groomed animals are well rested and prepared for the trip home. But despite the good care, the horses from the lead carriage are agitated, stomping their hooves, and whinnying nervously. Bram investigates.

The source of the problem is Esther's dog. Winston has slipped out the door and is yapping at the horses, repeatedly rushing toward them and backing away, taking care to stay out of kicking reach. Worse, Bram sees Esther, completely unsupervised, running as fast as her little legs can move, calling out to Winston in fear he will be harmed.

Jesse, too, had seen Esther a moment earlier and reacts instantly, racing to her rescue as the startled horses bolt into a run directly toward the child. It is clear neither Jesse nor Bram, who is running toward Esther from the opposite side, can reach the child quickly enough to sweep her up and jump out of the way in time to avoid the horses. If either is to save her, it will be Jesse because he is closer. Aware of the child's proximity to Bram, Jesse has just enough time to shout his name, grab Esther and loft her as high as he can in Bram's direction.

Falling to his knees to position his body under hers, Bram catches the screaming little girl as softly as he can, falling slowly backward to lessen the impact as much as possible. He succeeds; Esther suffers no harm other than being terrified.

The same, however, cannot be said for Jesse. As family members and friends watch in horror, the horse on the right veers away from Jesse but still hits him a hard glancing blow, spinning him to the ground. The metal rim of the front wheel breaks Jesse's outstretched forearm and the back wheel mangles his hand.

Screaming hysterically, Stephanie pushes aside everyone in her way, and without regard for modesty or decorum she kicks off her dancing shoes, jerks up her dress to free her legs for running, slides to the ground and clutches Jesse's head in her lap, all the while pleading for help.

"Jesse, oh, Jesse," she cries. "My darling, my love. Please, God, don't let him die."

Despite excruciating pain, Jesse, barely conscious, manages in the faintest of voices to utter: "Please, Stephanie, I'm OK. I'm OK."

But he is not. His injuries are serious. His arm is broken, his body badly bruised from the collision with the horse, and his hand in such a bloody state that Stephanie cannot even guess at the severity of the injury.

Frederick, dropping to his knees after rushing to Jesse's aid, has two realities register instantly in his mind. First, Stephanie loves Jesse, not him. Second, and much more urgent, he needs to act quickly and decisively as Dr. Carlisle.

He immediately takes charge, barking out a stream of orders. "Bram, you and the men carry Jesse to the couch in your father's office. Rufus, find me some pieces of wood I can use as splints on Jesse's arm. Mrs. Van Shelton, I need boiling water and plenty of clean towels. Ruben, fetch me my doctor's bag from the desk in my bedroom."

His orders are carried out as fast as the helpers can move. Having everything he requested, Frederick orders everyone out of the office except Bram, figuring correctly that Bram will not faint at what he will be required to do.

As Frederick skillfully sets about his tasks, Bram realizes he doesn't have to be a trained physician to see how he can help. He has set a number of bones when accidents happened on cattle drives. But Jesse's hand is another matter entirely. Half of the middle finger is gone, and two-thirds of his index finger is hanging on by little more than shreds of skin.

Frederick stanches the bleeding, cleans and repairs the hand as thoroughly as he can under the circumstances, and applies a thick bandage. Then he and Bram set Jesse's arm and attach splints from the wood Rufus has located and cut. Frederick manages to get enough laudanum into Jesse to put him into a less painful stupor. It is the best he can do away from a hospital in which he usually functions.

Turning to Bram, Frederick beckons him into the hallway where they break the news to the anxiously awaiting family members.

"Jesse's going to recover," he starts. "His life is not in danger. He's badly bruised, and his forearm is broken. Given time, he'll heal completely from those injuries. But his hand is another matter. It's his right hand, and parts of two fingers have been severed by the wagon wheels.

The women gasp in unison and begin to cry.

When they regain enough of their composure, Frederick continues. "I assure you that Jesse will regain full use of the rest of his hand, but he'll never again be able to use a pistol.

"He's resting reasonably comfortably because the medicine I gave him contains a strong narcotic. It will be at least tomorrow morning before he'll be conscious enough to talk, so, please, no visitors until then."

Bram pulls his father aside and informs him that he is going to use torches to make his way through the dark to the sheriff's house to head off the gunman who otherwise will show up at the ranch at daybreak.

"I know this sounds awful, so we'll keep it between you and me, Pa, but I'm taking along the cut off pieces of Jesse's fingers as proof. I don't want that gunslinger to have doubts about the truth of what happened here tonight." Mr. Van Shelton nods his agreement.

In the meantime, Mr. Van Shelton, with Ruben at his side, informs Stephanie, Mrs. Van Shelton, Lillian, and Frederick about Jesse's true identify. He slowly and deliberately provides detailed information to ensure they will have no doubt about the quality of Jesse's character after hearing about all the violence in which he has been involved.

Then, attempting to put everything that has happened into its proper perspective, Mr. Van Shelton concludes: "In one sense, it's tragic Jesse lost most of two fingers saving our precious Esther. But there's another way of looking at things. Because Jesse will never again be able to draw and shoot a handgun, J.D. Rohr can be allowed to 'die' and Jesse Bodine to live.

"He'll never again face pressure to leave us. Now he can make a permanent life with us on this ranch."

Still somewhat puzzled, Mrs. Van Shelton questions her husband. "I don't fully understand, dear. Just how does what's happened tonight resolve things for Jesse?"

"Let me put it another way, Marissa. Because there's no glory in outdrawing a man who has no trigger finger, the reputation-seekers will leave him alone. He can live a normal life now.

"Jesse, I'm sure, badly wanted the Almighty to help J.D. Rohr hide away at this ranch as Jesse Bodine so he wouldn't have to spend whatever he had left of his life being constantly on the move, fighting off one challenger after another until one of them bested him.

"The Good Lord answered his prayer with more finality. A whole J.D. Rohr would be pursued no matter what other name he took. Now with his trigger finger missing, J.D. Rohr was effectively killed off and Jesse Bodine survives.

"Call it divine intervention, my dear."

As the rest of the house falls quiet, Stephanie, at her insistence, spends the night in a chair at Jesse's bedside, her mind trying to arrange and categorize all the events and information of this extraordinary day and evening.

But, exhausted, she permits herself to periodically nod off. She awakens with the morning light to find Jesse staring at her with a curious grin on his face.

"I've been lying here for a time waiting for you to open your eyes," he says. "Please, Stephanie, while I'm still alert enough, let me speak. Did you mean all the things you said while I was lying on the ground last night? I mean about loving me? Wanting to be with me?"

"With all my heart, Jesse. I admit I've been terribly confused with Freddy here and all. But seeing you desperately hurt while saving my niece's life removed all my doubts.

"I don't know what I would have done if you had died. Jesse, I don't ever want us to be separated." And, somewhat embarrassed at her uncharacteristic candor, she adds teasingly: "Besides, where else will I find a better dancing partner?"

Though in constant pain, Jesse smiles broadly. "I'm not going anywhere, Stephanie. I'm going to stay right here on The Golden Eagle Ranch. I decided this morning that I'll earn my keep and provide for you and the family I hope we will have by breeding and raising quarter horses.

"The idea came to me out of nowhere this morning. We're going to raise the best there is—better than they do at the King Ranch in Texas. And what's more, we're going to make a lot of money selling our horses everywhere people raise cattle—everywhere in the world. I aim to earn my way into a full partnership on this ranch.

Stephanie is as grateful as she is pleased. Jesse's plan lifts their relationship over its biggest obstacles—her family's great wealth and Jesse's pride.

"Ironic, isn't it," Jesse muses. "All of these gunslingers would willingly give their left arm for J.D. Rohr's reputation, and God took my trigger finger to save me from mine. I just hope the name of J.D. Rohr will fade quickly away. If it's remembered at all, it should be for the reluctant gunfighter he was because that's the truth of it. "

That said, Jesse, aided by medication, slips into a peaceful sleep with the vision of the lovely Stephanie in his mind and a prayer of thanks to God on his lips.

Part 2

Three Years Later

The Transformation of Dr. Carlisle

"Frederick, the Good Lord saw fit to make you tall, handsome, intelligent, rich, popular, and gave you a noble profession. And that's not enough to make you happy!"

Chapter One

Profoundly Unhappy

Dr. Frederick Albert Carlisle sits thoughtfully at his ornately carved mahogany desk, elbows resting on the massive surface and hands clasped under his chin. From his position near the floor-to-ceiling windows on the second story, he looks down at the fashionably dressed passersby on Cambridge Street as they make their way to dinner at one of Boston's fine restaurants, or board their comfortably appointed carriages to return to their imposing houses where they will be pampered by staffs of meticulously trained servants.

Born into extravagant wealth, Frederick rarely notices his opulent trappings: The yellowish brown teak wood imported from India for the office floor and bookshelves. His exquisitely tailored suits and custom-made shoes whose combined cost equals a year's earnings for the average Boston physician. His house long recognized as one of the finest on Beacon Hill and a family treasure for generations. All of this luxury Frederick takes for granted, for he has always had it. From the moment of his birth, this son of Boston Brahmins has lacked for nothing that money can purchase or make possible.

And yet, on this chilly fall evening following a busy day of treating patients, Frederick feels hollow, numb, unable to lift himself from his chair and walk the twenty feet between the desk and the double-door entrance to his office. Despite his great wealth and his noble profession at which he excels, he is profoundly unhappy, and, after much effort and soul-searching, he is beginning to discover precisely why.

"Dr. Carlisle," Henrietta Johnston, the receptionist, says just above a whisper as she knocks politely and opens the door halfway. "Is it all right if I leave now?"

"Oh, of course, Mrs. Johnston. I lost track of the time. So sorry to have kept you waiting. Please, go ahead. I'll lock the office."

"Thank you, sir, and good evening to you."

As she starts to pull the door shut, Mrs. Johnston, a long-time employee, chances asking a question that has been worrying her for most of the week. "Begging your pardon, sir, but is there anything else I can do for you before I go? If you will forgive me for saying so, sir, you haven't seemed quite yourself."

"That's very kind of you, but, thank you, no. I'm fine. I have some things I'm trying to work out, but I am all right. I will see you tomorrow."

Resuming his train of thought, Frederick readily concedes that losing Stephanie Van Shelton to Jesse Bodine has something to do with his frame of mind. Of that he is certain. But that cannot be all of it. He is three years removed from his fateful trip to Nevada and the providential accident that cost Jesse his trigger finger but provoked the distraught Stephanie's confession of love.

No, there is more to it than that. Frederick believes he will always love Stephanie, but he has convinced himself that he no longer is *in love* with her. He is sensing a strong calling in his life, and he is struggling to come to terms with it. It dominates his thoughts but seems so illogical, so nonsensical, so foreign to all of his other life experiences that it is patently absurd.

But there it is, he realizes, as he pushes his chair away from his desk, stands slowly and pulls himself together. Since spending those four weeks pursuing Stephanie in Nevada, Frederick, a blue-blooded pillar of New England society, is gradually and unwittingly, but inexorably, being driven to a decision that will radically change his life.

Despite his disinclination to do so, Frederick, for the first time, is confronting the truth about the shallowness of his existence. Apart from the good work he does as a physician, his life is undeniably superficial. In all of his thirty-one years, he has never made a bed, or ironed a shirt, or shined a pair of shoes, or planted a flower, or cleaned a window, or bathed a pet, or babysat a child, or washed a single cup, glass, or dish.

He cannot even point to his good work as a physician as being above reproach, for his patients are wealthy, intelligent and articulate, scrupulously clean and pleasant smelling. The indigent, the homeless, the insane, the dirty and the foul-smelling—they are attended to by physicians of a lower rank.

To transform himself, presuming he has the will, Frederick faces one vexatious challenge: Honoria Lowell Blaire, his fiancé. His parents are dead, and he has no close relatives. As for his medical practice, Boston is full of other great physicians; his patients will not suffer. His large group of acquaintances will quickly adjust to his absence, and his small number of loyal and trustworthy friends will remain just that: loyal and trustworthy.

He isn't so sure about Honoria.

Not that there is anything suspiciously wrong with this young woman. And not that there is anything obviously remarkable about her either. Honoria seems a typical female member of a privileged family with a long New England pedigree: pretty, polished, socially skillful, graceful, well educated by the standards of her time, and prepared by years of careful tutoring to marry another wealthy member of her class and to perpetuate their way of life. She seems perfectly suited for the Frederick of old. The question is whether Honoria can—or more problematic, will be willing to—accommodate the transformed Frederick.

"I'll find out soon enough," Frederick says aloud in answer to his own thoughts as he exits the building to be greeted by Hamilton, his coachman.

"Are you making any stops along the way?" Hamilton inquires, "or should I drive straight home?" Hamilton has been with the Carlisle family since before Frederick's birth, closely observing the boy grow into a respected Boston physician. Years of familiarity have enabled Hamilton to read Frederick's moods, and he has been troubled of late about the young man's obvious distraction.

"No stops tonight, Hamilton. No patients to visit, thank goodness."

"Very well, sir. Cook has prepared a nice hot meal to be served on a tray in your library. We've filled the fireplace with wood so you can be warm and comfortable and enjoy your reading."

As he makes the short trip home in his Brougham Carriage, protected against the cold by lap robes and a metal foot warmer containing hot coals, Frederick ponders the next step in his plan. He has been thinking through the letter he will write to Mr. Van Shelton and Ruben, asking them to judge the soundness of his ideas and whether what he wants is doable. Frederick is confident these two good men will know best.

> *Dear Sirs:*
>
> *You undoubtedly will be shocked by the contents of this letter, but I assure you I am both in my right mind and absolutely serious. Gentlemen, I intend to make a change so drastic that you, as well as all others of my acquaintance, will find it most difficult to believe. I intend to give up my medical practice, sell the family home, leave my friends and move West. And I am determined to do so as soon as possible.*
>
> *I need your help.*

Please assess the need for another physician in Wyandotte and whether the doctor already there would be receptive to the idea. Please also check into the possibility of my acquiring a suitable building in town that could serve as both my home and my office, and whether I can locally hire or recruit at least one qualified nurse, a receptionist-bookkeeper, and a cook-house-keeper.

If all of these are doable, then I will need you to hire the appropriate craftsmen to do the necessary remodeling based upon requirements I will send you.

I would like this done as soon as possible.

I can only imagine the questions this letter arouses. All I can say for now is that I do not fully know the answers myself. But this I do know: My education and my skills as a physician and surgeon can be put to better use in Wyandotte, and my wealth eliminates the need for my practice to be financially profitable. I want my life to count for more than it has up to this point.

With warmest regards and best wishes to the entire family, I am gratefully yours,

> *Frederick*

He posts the letter the following morning before talking over his plans with anyone—including Honoria. She will be told tonight. "It will be a shock to her, of that I am certain," Frederick admits to himself. "But I'll find out for sure what she loves and values most—the life to which she is accustomed or a life, whatever it may be, with the man for whom she has both privately and publicly expressed her love."

Chapter Two

The Van Shelton Family Reacts

Mr. Van Shelton and Ruben stare at each other across the big desk in their office at The Golden Eagle Ranch. The shock of Dr. Carlisle's letter has rendered them speechless. Freddy, as the family calls him, has written several times before, so getting a letter from him is not surprising. But of all the information one of his letters might contain, his announcement of plans to move to their small town is so astounding its effect is stunning.

"Do you think he's really means it?" Ruben finally manages to blurt out, loosening his blue-and-green striped tie and exhaling noisily.

"I suspect so," his father replies, throwing up both hands to signal he is just as taken aback as his son. "Freddy is an exceptionally intelligent and rational man. I take him at his word."

"Well, then, we have some work to do," Ruben says, his equally rational mind already sorting out the details for complying with the requests Frederick has stipulated. "And we need to work as fast as is reasonable. Freddy clearly is anxious about the feasibility of his plan and eager to implement it."

"Good," Mr. Van Shelton nods in agreement. "Let's share Freddy's letter with your mother, Lillian, Stephanie, and Jesse over dinner tonight." Then grinning in anticipation of reading their faces when they hear the news, Mr. Van Shelton cautions: "On second thought, Ruben, perhaps we had better wait until dessert is served. Their reaction upon hearing the news just might put them off their feed."

Two hours later, Mr. Van Shelton gets an eyeful. Stephanie shrieks with delight. Lillian immediately pictures how stimulating it would be to have someone of her New England background and upbringing with whom to converse. Mrs. Van Shelton seems puzzled, as she always does at the prospect of change that might affect the routine of her life. As for Jesse, he struggles to present an impartial reaction, but he feels as if he has just been kicked squarely in the gut by one of his prized quarter horses.

"Oh, my goodness!" Stephanie shouts exuberantly. "This is so wonderful. I don't understand it at all, but it's wonderful just the same." Then rising from her chair and pointing one index finger at Lillian and the other toward her mother, Stephanie exclaims: "When word gets out, every single woman in this territory is going to find herself suddenly sick enough to be his first patient. Why, we're just liable to have an instantaneous epidemic in Wyandotte."

Jesse doesn't hear anyone's reply. He is pondering whether he'll be safe in letting go of the jealously he felt moments earlier at the news that his wife's handsome former suitor will be frequently in her presence again. "Damn it, man," he chastises himself, for he both likes and admires Freddy, especially for coming to his aid within seconds after the accident that took two of his fingers, and, at least indirectly, cost Freddy a future with Stephanie.

"I hope that's not the case," Lillian interjects. "A stampede of women with matrimony on their minds just might persuade Freddy to catch the next stagecoach back East," she jokes. "Besides, Stephanie, aren't you forgetting he's engaged to Honoria Lowell Blaire?"

"Oh, her," Stephanie replies in dismissal. "You can forget about her. There's no way she will ever leave a big city where she lives like nobility."

"I did," Lillian sharply reminds the family, turning her head to glance at each person at the table.

Sensing a moment of awkwardness, Mr. Van Shelton looks at his wife and observes: "You haven't said anything, Marissa. What do you make of all this?"

"I don't . . . I don't know what to think," she stammers, her confusion punctuated by worry lines crowding for room on her forehead. "Not just yet anyway. I need time to mull this over. But don't get me wrong, any of you. He's a delightful man, and we can certainly use his professional skills in our little community."

"Well," Mr. Van Shelton chuckles with a quick wink in Ruben's direction, "anyone for dessert?"

***

Mr. Van Shelton, Ruben, and Jesse join forces the next day to start carrying out Frederick's requests. Mr. Van Shelton knows the owner of every building in Wyandotte, so he will work on finding a suitable structure. Ruben will attend to the legal details. And Jesse, who has the construction and carpentry skills to convert a building into an office-home, will assess both the potential and the costs.

They agree what they choose must be in on near the town to make it as accessible as possible for patients, and they want a two-story building that will enable Dr. Carlisle to conduct his practice on the first level while having the privacy of the upstairs to himself. The building must be large enough to accommodate a combined reception area and waiting room, an office, an examination area, and a surgery. The upstairs will require a small kitchen, at least one bedroom and bath, and a living room.

Mr. Van Shelton rejects the first three buildings he inspects as each fails, for one reason or another, to meet the minimum requirements. The fourth he believes has promise. So he joins Ruben and Jesse for lunch at The Silver Queen Hotel, which, despite its royal name, features simple fare provided by a good cook.

"If I weren't so danged hungry, I'd take you two directly to the building I think just might do," the older man says, helping himself to another pork chop and a heaping spoonful of mashed potatoes. "It's not so much a building as it is a house," he explains. "I mean it's never had a commercial use. Old Man Hollister, the banker in these parts for a long time before he died a few years ago, built a fine house just on the outskirts of town, and it's unoccupied. Nice two-story wooden structure with a stone base. You've been in that house, haven't you, Ruben?"

"Yes, father. But not since I was a teenager, so I don't remember much about the inside. Except that it is big. And it has to be pretty big to suit Freddy's needs. But, you know, it just might do, except I am concerned about how it has weathered after being unoccupied for some time. Do you have the key, or is someone going to show the place to us?"

"I've got the key. The bank owns the place now, so Chet Willowbee—he's the president of the bank, Jesse—gave us permission to keep the key as long as we need it. He didn't have to be told the three of us aren't going to have the final say. Besides, I want to know how suitable our ladies envision the place to be. I mean, we can figure out the physical possibilities and needs all right, but the women will want to oversee the furnishings, especially for the living quarters.

"But I sure would admire some coffee and apple pie before walking over there. We've waited this long, so fifteen minutes more won't hurt anything. Besides," he realizes with obvious satisfaction, "Marissa's not here to remind me that my weight is getting out of hand again. So, this will just be our little secret," he grins in the manner of a small boy sneaking a fingertip's worth of icing from a cake his mother has set aside for dinner.

Chapter Three

Frederick Confronts Honoria

Blissfully unaware of what her fiancé is dead set on telling her in just a few hours, Honoria Lowell Blaire goes methodically about her preparations for marriage to one of the most sought-after bachelors in New England. She and her mother have already made arrangements with the minister of the historic King's Chapel, a church whose bell is linked to Paul Revere and whose cemetery is the oldest in Boston. They also have arranged for the printing of the wedding invitations, visited one of the city's finest dressmakers, contracted the services of a prominent baker, hired musicians, ordered flowers, and attended to myriad other details.

Honoria feels as if she is in a dream state. She is experiencing everything a bride could hope or wish for; yet, like most humans in such rare moments, she is not fully accepting that anything so good can be real.

Euphoria, she will soon discover, can be traitorous and cruelly brief.

***

Frederick is dumbfounded by Honoria's reaction to his explanation. He has spoken with sincerity, honesty, and kindness, holding Honoria's left hand tenderly in his right and looking her squarely in her eyes. But the more he says, the colder her trembling fingers become. He was prepared for tears, disbelief, protestations, anger. He had rehearsed consoling statements for every reaction he could envision. Not a single one is appropriate. He has misjudged Honoria—extraordinarily badly. It is as if he doesn't really know this woman with whom he has pledged to spend the rest of his life. So he says nothing else. Just waits and listens.

Honoria, who thus far has not offered a single syllable, finally speaks: "Give me one hour alone please, Frederick. Just one hour. Then I'll return to this room and we will talk." That is all she can manage. She feels faint as she swiftly exits the room, shaken to her core. Honoria musters all of her self-control and dignity to keep from sobbing. That she will not do—not in front of Frederick or any other man. She will cry. But crying is something she does alone. And has since becoming a woman.

"Frederick doesn't really know me," Honoria realizes. "But neither does anyone else, so I really can't blame him."

Honoria concedes she appears to be just another typical young female of her class and social standing. Her situation in life is dictated by rigid expectations and conventions, so that's the way she lives. It is not who she is; it is who she is expected to be. Inwardly she is someone else, but no one else knows and only her father and a couple of admiring friends have suspicions.

Good breeding, fine manners, and intelligence are in ample supply in her social circle. But Honoria has something infinitely more valuable. Honoria has wisdom. She learned years earlier to differentiate between intelligence and wisdom. The former meaning the ability to learn, to catch on quickly, and to acquire information; the latter, however, being defined by insight, perception, and good judgment. She has long realized that many are intelligent, but few are wise.

In the hour she asked for, she deals with the "why" and tries to understand how Frederick can even consider such a polar-opposite life. He has not rejected her. He has not broken their engagement. Actually, he reassured her of his love and asked her to join him, fully appreciating what a bewildering and frightening change that would present for her.

She is surprised, hurt, feels at least somewhat mistreated, perhaps betrayed. But she is determined to speak rationally to Frederick, even though she knows she cannot—and will not—suppress all of her emotions. She must gather her thoughts so she cannot merely make herself understood, but also make certain she will not be misunderstood. She allows herself forty-five minutes.

***

Honoria feels reasonably composed when she re-enters the room where Frederick is pacing nervously and looking painfully concerned. She hoped he would appear at least a little impatient with her or eager to leave. His obvious compassion for the ordeal he is putting her through causes tears to escape her eyes—something she had steeled herself against happening.

"Frederick," she begins, "please permit me to have my say without interruption. I promise to listen to everything you have to tell me afterward."

"Of course, Honoria. Take all the time you need."

"First, Frederick, I couldn't have been more surprised if you had told me you plan to have yourself tattooed all over and put on display in a traveling carnival."

Now it is Frederick's turn to be surprised. Despite the seriousness of the situation, he finds himself amused by her analogy. He cannot recall her ever before saying anything remotely humorous.

Honoria manages a trace of a smile, too. "I didn't realize until tonight we really don't know each other—sort of like a couple in an arranged marriage. Our families have known each other for generations. We belong to a privileged class, we have powerful social and political connections, and we both know how to live in that world.

"I admire you for the good person you are, and I dare suggest you feel the same about me. I very much appreciate that you have become a physician instead of choosing the self-indulgent lifestyle so many of our peers are living. I believe you would make an attentive, loyal, and considerate husband and a loving father. I believe I would be the same kind of wife.

"I love you, and I am confident in your love for me. *But,*" she emphasizes, "what our relationship is almost completely devoid of—if you will pardon my perhaps inappropriate candor—is any passion. In other words, Frederick, each of us is 'settling' on a spouse. You are thirty-one and want a family; I am twenty-three, several years older than my married contemporaries, and you are a great catch. I didn't marry earlier because most young men of our class still act like adolescents. That I could not abide in a husband.

"Don't misunderstand, please. I could be passionately in love with you if you had demonstrated a similar feeling for me. But you have not, and I know you do not feel that way. You were passionately in love with Stephanie but lost her. Now you are 'settling' for me.

"So, do as you wish, Frederick. Renounce the life you have always had, pack up, and go to Nevada, and see how it works out. I have only two requests: Wait a year before you sell your family house, and give the two of us that much time to correspond and figure out how we feel at that later point.

"Why? Because as much as you have hurt me tonight, I find your behavior oddly exciting. You may be a much more interesting man than I thought. You apparently have adventure in your soul and a willingness to take risks for something you feel deeply about. I think you also are seeing there is more to me than you previously thought. During our courtship, I fear I misled you. I have played the role society has devised and I thought you expected in a prospective wife."

Honoria locks unblinking eyes with Frederick, and finally says: "All right, Frederick, I've had my say. Now it's your turn, and I want you to be as honest and as revealing as I have been—no matter how painful for me or for you."

Frederick rises from his chair, stuffs his hands into the pockets of his trousers while appearing to investigate the ceiling from corner to corner. Finally, after a pause so long it embarrasses him, he manages to speak. "Honoria, I don't think I'll sleep well tonight. Maybe not for several nights. Tonight has not gone at all as I had envisioned. It puzzles me. And you—well, you are the biggest mystery of all.

"You've made me realize we truly do not know each other. First, I must apologize for not treating you as an intellectual equal. I didn't recognize previously why, as you just explained, you have acted as superficially as most of the other young women of our acquaintance. I have much more respect for you after what has transpired between us tonight, and I, too, find the 'new you' inexplicably more interesting and exciting.

"I thought you would either faint, sob uncontrollably, or throw your engagement ring in my face and stomp out the door and out of my life. Now I find I am glad you didn't. But, Honoria, I'm still going to Nevada. I just have to. As I told the Van Sheltons in my explanation to them, I want to be of more use, to have my life count for more than it has up until now. But I will honor your requests about the house and our staying in touch. You're right in saying I might change my mind. I have my doubts, too.

"Now, how do we want to handle this so you are not publicly embarrassed by my leaving and your family and our friends don't make some kind of scandal out of all this?"

"I'll take care of it," Honoria assures without hesitation. "Now that you know I am 'intellectually' capable of dealing with such matters, just leave it to me. When are you going?"

"Day after tomorrow," Frederick answers. "I will write frequently."

"As will I," Honoria pledges.

Chapter Four

The Journey Begins

Frederick stares blankly through the train's private compartment window as he begins the first leg of his journey westward. He is not enjoying the trip, and the disappointment gnaws on him. For months he has anticipated starting his new life on a totally fresh basis, having cut all ties with Boston—his home, his medical practice, his friends and associates—and, yes, even Honoria.

He figured the chances of her foregoing the only life she has ever known and joining him in his transformation were all but nil. She caught him off guard with her request that he not sell his house for a year and give them a chance to discover if they still want to get married at the end of that time.

He vacillates between being resentful about leaving with strings still attached to the city and to Honoria and departing a totally free man. Even worse, he cannot get the woman off his mind. Their parting embrace was unlike any other they had previously shared. She had pressed her body fully against his for the first time in their relationship. And he liked it. Far too much.

His destination is a long way off, but at least, he reasons with some satisfaction, the medical equipment and supplies he shipped from Boston will arrive ahead of him.

"Bram and some of his ranch hands will see that everything is picked up at the freight office," Mr. Van Shelton's letter has assured Frederick. "They'll have it unpacked and waiting for you at the house Ruben, Jesse, and I purchased in your name. Don't worry about a thing, my boy; if we have overlooked anything, we'll make it right as soon as you settle in."

Frederick knows Jesse and the crew he hired will have the requested renovations completed, and Mrs. Van Shelton, Stephanie, and Lillian will have the living quarters furnished and decorated to the finest detail. "All I have to do is arrive in the right frame of mind," Frederick lectures himself.

He manages a wry smile at the thought of what his insightful and loving mother would think about his mood if she were still alive. He could almost hear her say: "Frederick, the Good Lord saw fit to make you tall, handsome, intelligent, rich, popular, and gave you a noble profession. *And that's not enough to make you happy!*"

"Better get myself together. I have much to ponder. It's a long trip, and there is plenty to be done when I get to Wyandotte."

***

In Ruben's letter informing Frederick that an appropriate building has been found, he also assures his friend he will not be involving himself in any professional conflicts. Wyandotte has only one physician, the man Frederick met briefly in his previous visit. His name is Cornelius Valens Haggerty, known simply as "Doc" to avoid the name branded on him by his father, an enthusiast in the history of the Roman Empire.

"Be glad to have another doctor around here," Doc says on being informed of Frederick's plans and concerns. "I liked him immediately when he visited a few years back, and I certainly can use the help. Besides, I suspect that Harvard medical education means this lad has a lot he can teach me about the latest advancements in the field. And on the other hand, I know danged well that a big city doctor is going to need a bunch of help in adjusting to practicing in a little country town with no hospital."

Chuckling, Doc adds as he shifts his eyes to take in the Van Shelton men, "Bet Dr. Carlisle has never gone to a ranch to deliver a baby and gets recruited to help with a calf-pulling before leaving."

"No," an amused Mr. Van Shelton assures. "I don't imagine there's a whole lot of that going on in downtown Boston. Freddy will indeed need all the help you can give him in that regard, Doc."

"Seriously," Doc cautions, "I have real concerns about anybody like Dr. Carlisle adjusting to such a radical change. But I want all three of you—Vincent, Ruben, and Jesse—to be assured that I will do all I can to help him along.

"I'll take him on my calls, introduce him around to the folks, and give him every opportunity to observe just how life is lived in these parts."

"Appreciate that, Doc," Mr. Van Shelton replies. "Your efforts will not be wasted; I assure you. Freddy's serious. He'll give it his all."

"Good to know," Doc allows. "Good to know because an upper-class New England doctor is certainly a fish out of water around here. He will have to be patient and work very hard to gain people's trust, you know. Wish it weren't so, but that's the way it is, I'm afraid.

"It will help him right off that he likes to dress western, according to what Bram tells me. At least he won't look so different when folks size him up. But it won't help at all that he doesn't speak our language."

"What do you mean by that?" Ruben objects, irritated because his wife sounds just like Frederick. "Are you referring to his good grammar? His accent? That he might sound snooty? What?"

"All of that, I suppose, Ruben. And meaning no offense to Dr. Carlisle or to Lillian. It's just the locals aren't accustomed to hearing r's dropped out of words. You know, 'hot' instead of heart, 'wud' instead of word, and 'god' instead of guard. Then, too, hearing r's added at the ends of words like 'idea,' 'saw,' and 'Virginia" is going to sound mighty strange, too."

"C'mon, Doc!" Ruben exclaims. "You don't really believe that, do you?"

"'Fraid I do, Ruben. Of course, in fairness to Dr. Carlisle, our twang and our habit of droppin' g's' at the end of words is going to take a little getting used to as well. At any rate, he won't be automatically accepted even with your family's support and mine."

"Well," Mr. Van Shelton interjects with a note of finality, "once he starts making people feel better, and especially after he cures a few of their children, they'll be so grateful they won't give a hoot where he comes from or what he sounds like."

***

The gloom that had gripped Frederick from the beginning of his journey starts to loosen its hold once he reaches the western side of the Mississippi. That mighty river somehow serves to provide both a physical and a psychological divide between his past and his future, securing them in place as if they were two separate and distinct lifetimes.

It helps too, that Frederick has shed his eastern clothes for the western garb Bram picked out for him on Frederick's previous trip three years back. "I might not be a genuine westerner yet, but by damn I'm at least going to look like one," he vows.

Frederick especially loves the rich leather boots, the wide-brimmed Stetson hat, and the broad belt with western floral tooling and big turquoise buckle. And when he strides through the dining car a little while later, he draws admiring glances from the men as well as the women.

At six-foot, three inches tall, Frederick always stands out. His lean, muscular body rivals the physique of a seasoned cowboy. Altogether,

Frederick is extraordinarily handsome. Not pretty, mind you, thoroughly masculine with heavy dark, wavy hair, thick expressive eyebrows, prominent cheekbones, and a strong jaw line. And perhaps just to torment other males and to further stir the passions of admiring women, Mother Nature crafted Frederick a beautiful set of strong teeth, a couple of deep-set dimples, and such light blue eyes that the ladies can see their reflections in them.

Frederick's mother was right: He has it all—in abundance.

Chapter Five

An Immediate Call to Action

Doc Haggerty is unexpectedly among those awaiting the stage bringing Frederick to Wyandotte. He was not invited by Mr. Van Shelton, Ruben, or Jesse, who arrived earlier. Not that Doc wouldn't be welcome as part of Frederick's reception or that he himself had planned to be there.

No, Doc has a special reason. An urgent one, in fact. One of the Turner boys at the family ranch about ten miles outside of town was thrown off a bronco he was attempting to break earlier in the morning and was stomped in the back. Sixteen-year-old Preston Turner is in danger of being permanently paralyzed, and Doc wants Frederick to help him determine how to prevent that, if possible. The weary traveler, it appears, will be greeted as Frederick only momentarily. Instead, it will be Dr. Carlisle emerging to be put to the test immediately.

Because his trip by stagecoach was neither comfortable nor restful, Frederick was looking forward to having his feet on the ground again and enjoying a leisurely meal with his friends, followed soon afterward by an early retirement. However, after a hasty greeting, Doc informs his new colleague he will get neither. The two physicians promptly set out for the Turner ranch in Doc's two-seater carriage.

"Have you seen the boy yet?" Frederick inquires.

"No, Dr. Carlisle, I have not. The ranch foreman who rode in to get me less than an hour ago said Preston is alert and talking but in considerable pain. First thing we'll need to do is assess his chances for living and do all we can in that regard. Then we can try to determine if he will be able to use his legs again."

"That will be a challenge for sure, Doc," Frederick allows. "I haven't treated many accidents involving horses, but I have seen my share of bad falls resulting in back injuries. I've never found the extent of the damage easy to diagnose."

"Like as not only time will tell," Doc agrees. "Meanwhile, Dr. Carlisle, let me take total responsibility in this case, even if we end up following a diagnosis and treatment you recommend. It would not do at all for you to get off to a bad start with the folks. If this turns out badly, as it likely will, I'm trusted enough not to be blamed. After all, I delivered that boy and each of his parents as well."

"Wise advice, Doc; I'll just follow your lead. And, by the way, please call me Frederick. I hope to be a friend as well as a colleague."

"Good," Doc replies. "But I'll call you Dr. Carlisle in all professional circumstances, if you don't mind. I want people around here to regard you as a well-educated physician with special skills and talents. That will be an important part of your acceptance."

"I defer to your experience and judgment," Frederick says. "You know the people and the western way of life, and I very much appreciate your acceptance of me—especially considering you barely know me."

***

The doctors withhold pain medication, even though young Preston is sorely in need of it. They have to get all the information they can from him before he sleeps.

His back is a mess, severely cut and bruised by the horse's hooves. Preston can move his upper body—head, neck, arms and hands. But his anxious parents have detected no response from either leg. Preston feels pain only from the waist up. The outlook appears grim.

After shooing the protesting parents out of the room, Doc and Frederick examine the boy, speaking in hushed tones so as not to be overheard. They detect no obvious signs of serious bleeding, externally or internally. But they are unable to determine for certain how badly the spine is damaged. They do, however, find three broken ribs. Thankfully, both Doc and Frederick conclude the boy's life is not in danger, unless something unexpected turns up when the swelling subsides enough for them to make a more accurate inspection.

So they clean the boy's wounds, stitch the deep cuts, and bandage his ribs. Now the waiting begins. While Frederick remains silent as he has been advised, Doc informs the Turner family of his assessment, tells them to keep Preston secured in bed and to feed him broth anytime he can take it. Doc also carefully instructs them of the dosage and times for giving the boy the painkiller that will allow him to rest. He promises to return the next day.

Mrs. Turner assures Doc she will follow his instructions to the letter as Doc continues to do all the talking while Frederick patiently listens. The Turners ask no more questions and thank both men for coming. They say nothing else to Dr. Carlisle, for they quite obviously are not about to put their son's care and future into the hands of an outsider.

By the time they make their way back to Wyandotte, it is too late and too dark for Frederick to look over his office and lodgings. The town's deputy sheriff, Aaron Brinkley, escorts Frederick to the house, having insisted a few hours earlier the Van Sheltons start for home before they ran out of daylight. Frederick finds the meal the Van Sheltons thoughtfully left for him, and after eating most of it, the exhausted newcomer goes directly to bed.

There will be time enough the next day to tour the premises and have lunch with his friends, who left word with the deputy that they will send a carriage for him at noon. The stagecoach ride, followed by the twenty-mile round trip by horse and carriage to the Turner ranch works like a sedative for Frederick, who sleeps the night through.

Chapter Six

Settling In

Awakened by sunlight beaming strongly through the bedroom window whose shade had not been lowered, Frederick finds himself in surroundings so unfamiliar he wonders for a moment just where in the world he is. Gradually, it comes to him: He is in the second day of his new life.

Frederick checks the time, surprised at the lateness of the hour. It is 10:13 a.m., more than three hours past his usual rising time. He glances at himself in the mirror as he enters his bathroom. "That guy could use a close shave and a good thorough bath," he reckons as if talking to another person. Surely that haggard face and mop of wavy hair couldn't belong to him. The long trip, topped off by the medical visit to the Turner place, has indeed taken its toll.

Cleanup, however, will have to wait. Frederick is too eager to check out his place. He spends a good hour walking from room to room upstairs and down taking in every detail of the personal furnishings and the medical equipment and supplies. "The Van Sheltons and the Bodines did their jobs well," he admires. He is glad he overspent on the presents he brought each of them from Boston. "They deserve those, and more," he concludes appreciatively.

"Dammit," Frederick mutters, scolding himself for cutting the time so closely between his rising and the arrival of the carriage sent by the Van Sheltons. He wants to look his best when he reunites with the family, but he will have to hurry. He has plenty of clean western clothing at the ready, so all he needs is a shave and a good washing.

Frederick keeps the carriage and its driver waiting an extra half hour, not realizing it is Bram who volunteered to pick him up, and Bram is the least patient of the Van Sheltons.

"What the hell kept you, man," Bram says by way of a greeting. "If I'da known you was gonna be primpin' so long, I coulda stopped off at the Gentleman's Club for a quick round with one of the ladies."

Frederick is relieved Bram isn't really angry. Somehow, they hit it off three years earlier when Bram admired how the greenhorn from the east had gamely, if ineptly, tried his hand at roping, branding, sleeping out under the stars, and eating chuck wagon food—qualities Bram appreciates in a man. From the start, Frederick was impressed with Bram's fearlessness and penchant for speaking his mind. "A man never has to guess where he stands with Bram," Frederick reasons.

"Glad to see you held onto the Nevada clothes I picked out for you," Bram compliments as they board the carriage for the trip to the ranch. "Looks one helluva lot better than those sissy suits you and Ruben are used to wearin'. S'pose you brought those along, too?"

"Only a couple, Bram," Frederick admits. "Just in case your mother organizes another dance party or you decide to make an honest woman out of one of your favorites at the Gentleman's Club."

"You a doctor or a comedian?" Bram retorts.

Abruptly changing the tone of the conversation, Bram rearranges his grip on the reins, turns to Frederick and asks point blank: "Not that I mind your company, but just what the shit are you doin' in Nevada, Freddie? I didn't believe it when my pa first told me about it, and I'm still havin' trouble turnin' it over in my mind. I mean, if Stephanie was still single, that'd be a reason I'd understand. I'd purely like to know."

"I think you already do, Bram. Or at least you've been told, I suspect. I made it clear in my letters. It just boils down to wanting to do more good with my life than I was accomplishing in Boston. My rich patients didn't really need me. Ordinary people, especially the poor, do. Furthermore, I could not make that kind of change there. No one in the circle my family has belonged to for generations would ever have accepted my exclusively serving the needy in the slum areas of Boston. It's as simple as that. Honest."

"Good enough for me, Freddy," Bram allows. "What you call ordinary people, well, around here those kinds of folks trust me because they know I'm more like them than I am my own family. So, anything I can do . . . ."

"I'll rely on that, Bram. My experience at the Turner ranch yesterday made it clear I am seen as an outsider. They weren't rude, you understand; but it will be a long time, if ever, before they accept me they way they do Doc Haggerty."

"True, Freddy, but I'm positive I can help. I'll drop a word here and there with my ranch hands and their families. People will come around when my friends turn to you for doctorin'.

"By the way, how is the Turner boy?"

"Too early to tell, Bram. But it doesn't look good. Doc and I are hoping that when the swelling subsides, Preston will get the feeling back in his legs. But the odds are against it."

"Damn shame," Bram says. "Preston's one of the best of the young men around here. He's got Ruben's brains and my skills at ranchin'. But if he ends up crippled, it's gonna kill his pa. The family's countin' on Preston to run things."

***

Frederick's welcome when he and Bram arrive at the ranch is genuine and heart-warming, giving him the reassurance he needs to believe he is making the right move. Firm handshakes accompanied by pats on the back from Mr. Van Shelton, Ruben, and Jesse. Hugs from Mrs. Van Shelton, Lillian, and Stephanie. And a rehearsed but sincere greeting from Ruben and Lillian's children, Jonathan and Esther. For the next few hours, Frederick can put everything else aside and thoroughly enjoy the good food and loving company of friends who treat him like family.

"So when do you plan to open your office?" Lillian inquires as Frederick is cutting into a steak so rare it is practically mooing.

"Well," he says after he has taken his first bite, "I'm meeting with my three employees tomorrow morning. If all goes well, I'll hang out my shingle the next day and see what happens."

"Freddy, I took the liberty of having some handbills printed, and, with your permission, I'll have a couple of boys pass them out and hang them in store windows," Stephanie announces proudly. "Oh," she chuckles, "don't worry, Freddy. They are very professionally worded. I won't make you look like a drummer with pots and pans to sell."

Sensing a pause on Lillian's and Stephanie's part, Mrs. Van Shelton, who has patiently been awaiting her turn to speak, looks earnestly at Frederick and asks if the building and furnishings are to his liking.

"Couldn't be better, Mrs. Van Shelton. Everything looks perfect. The men did a great job in picking out the property and overlooking the remodeling, and you women just outdid yourselves with the furnishings and the decorations. I think I have everything I need except patients."

"They'll come along, Freddy; don't you fret any about that," Mr. Van Shelton assures while piling more food on his plate, over the objections of his wife. "We've circulated the word about you, and so has Doc Haggerty. "May be slow at first, but that'll give you some extra time to get your bearings around here."

"Dr. Freddy, is it all right if I ask you something," sweet Esther inquires, looking at her parents for a nod of permission.

"Of course, sweetheart," Frederick smiles. "You go ahead and ask me anything you like."

"I was just wondering—that is, if you can stay a while longer—if you will play with me and Winston? You remember him, don't you? My little dog?"

"Sure, honey, just as soon as we finish our dinner."

"And will you dance with me, too, the way you did when you visited us when I was little?"

"I'm all yours, Esther. As I recall, you have your grandmother's talent for dancing. Maybe we can persuade her to dance with us, too. What do you say to that?"

"Oh, that would be wonderful, Dr. Freddie."

Not to be outdone by his younger sister, Jonathan pipes in with an invitation for a ride on a couple of his grandfather's prized horses, and Frederick agrees to that, too.

Altogether, it is a wonderful afternoon. With one exception. Frederick thinks he detects a slight uneasiness between Stephanie and Jesse. Nothing he can put his finger on. And it could be just his imagination. Still, he finds it a little disconcerting, so he tucks the thought away to enjoy the rest of his reunion with his dear friends.

His suspicions, however, reappear as he and the family are saying their goodbyes. Stephanie slips a note into his jacket pocket while whispering in a barely audible voice: "I need to talk to you—privately."

When Frederick is safely out of sight of the ranch, he retrieves the note and reads: "I'll be in town Wednesday afternoon. Unless you send word to the contrary, I'll drop by your office with some flowers on the pretext of adding a finishing touch to your living quarters."

"Puzzling," Frederick thinks.

Chapter Seven

Doc's "Wicked" Surprise

Another note is awaiting Frederick when he returns home just before dusk. Signed by Doc Haggerty, it is attached to the front door and reveals this message: "Need your help. I'll call for you at 7 a.m. Explanation to follow."

"That's rather strange," Frederick observes. "Wonder why Doc is being so mysterious? Guess I'll find out in the morning," he says, folding the note away in the same pocket as Stephanie's.

Frederick feels stuffed. "Way too much to eat and drink," he scolds himself. "Good thing they don't invite me every day." The meal, the pleasant company, and the ride home have made Frederick sleepy, but he is determined to finish writing specific job descriptions and instructions for each of his three employees before meeting with them at noon the next day. He started the project on the train West, but finishing them will take at least two hours.

The rich food and the concentration needed to finish the notes make it difficult for Frederick to wind down sufficiently to promote a restful sleep. So Doc's knock on the door at promptly 7 a.m. seems several hours premature. It takes two cups of black coffee at breakfast at the hotel and Doc's refusal to reveal the source of the call to rouse Frederick's brain from its stupor.

"I'm not sure I like that smirk on your face, Doc," Frederick challenges. "Something tells me you have a wicked streak."

"We'll see, Frederick; we'll see," Doc teases. So the two physicians turn their attention to a hearty meal of biscuits, ham and eggs, and fried apples."

Finally, Doc is ready for them to take a leisurely stroll to wherever it is he intends to guide them. Walking to a back street in an unfashionable part of town, they stop in front of a two-story wooden building with a shabby exterior needing paint, but with an inexplicably pristine sign proclaiming this to be the home of the infamous "Gentlemen's Club."

"Doc!" Frederick exclaims in total surprise. "Surely this is not where you are taking me."

"Oh, for heaven's sake, Frederick," Doc chides. "I didn't bring you here for, uh, recreation. I examine 'The Girls' every month, and today's the day. You need to get to know all my patients, especially the types not included among your clientele in Boston. Come on in and I'll introduce you around."

The interior of the Gentlemen's Club is a remarkable contrast to the front. It is garish to be sure, but the décor is not inexpensive. It features a piano, a bar, fiery red wallpaper with a flowery pattern that clashes with the purple carpet, and oversized couches and chairs. Frederick not only has never seen anything like it, he has never even imagined it. Not that he is prudish; he visited a few such establishments in Europe when he took The Grand Tour after graduating from college, but they were tasteful, the "ladies" were refined, and they came with prices no cowpoke or storekeeper in Wyandotte could afford.

"Ah, here comes our charming hostess, Contessa Bianca," Doc announces with a flair. Frederick shifts his eyes toward the wide staircase being descended by a tall, elegantly dressed middle-aged woman with a seductive figure—large breasts, a small waist, and a lustfully round bottom. But that's not what causes Frederick's jaw to drop in a silent gasp. Contessa Bianca is an albino—the first he has ever seen outside of a textbook. Doc, Frederick can plainly tell, is enjoying his surprise immensely.

The Contessa, as she insists on being called, has chalk-white skin and hair. Her only natural color is a reddish tint to her eyes, about half as red as her lipstick. She wears heavy makeup in varying shades of gray and black, giving her a strikingly bizarre presentation.

"Whoa!" Frederick whispers to Doc.

"Whoa, indeed!" Doc concurs.

"Who's your gorgeous friend, Doc?" the Contessa inquires in a sultry tone. "Little early in the day to be bringing him around, don't you think?"

"Oh no, Contessa. He's not here for that. He's the new doctor in town. Name's Frederick Carlisle. I brought him to help me examine the girls."

"Oh my, this is one morning I don't think my girls will resent rising early. They are going to love 'Dr. Gorgeous,'" she chuckles, giving Frederick a thorough examination with her eyes.

"Come on to the back of the house, gentlemen. The girls are waiting."

When they enter the private dining area where the girls are gathered, they observe five silent women waiting unenthusiastically for an examination each would just as soon do without. They are tired, sleepy and look as if they'd gone to bed after coming out losers in a free-for-all brawl.

"All right, girls! Wake up! Look alive! Doc's here," the Contessa shouts, making the circuit around the room and giving each girl a good shaking.

They look up at Doc with neither a smile nor a greeting. But when their eyes focus sufficiently to see the handsome, well-groomed stranger, they sit up, take notice and flee the room as a group.

"What the hell?" Doc utters bewilderedly.

The Contessa laughs heartily. "They'll be back in about fifteen minutes after they've brushed their hair, put on some makeup and picked out something more enticing to wear. I think Dr. Gorgeous made an impression."

And almost fifteen minutes to the second, in they come, looking as the Contessa had predicted.

"Girls, I want you to meet Dr. Carlisle. He's new in town and is giving Doc a hand with the examinations."

"He can give me a hand, or anything else, anytime he wants," the lone black member of the group, interjects, barely getting the words out before several "Me, toos" are offered by a few others.

"Now, ladies, please mind what little manners you have. Dr. Carlisle is not here for entertainment. Let me introduce you, so these two busy doctors can get on with their work." The Contessa prides herself on having an eclectic, if not unique, selection of employees. An albino madam, she reasons, shouldn't be the only unconventional member of the establishment.

"The 'shy' one who just propositioned you calls herself Mustang Maggie. I'll leave the name to your imagination. Next to her is a Japanese gal I brought in from San Francisco. A sailor riding through town decided after passing some time with her that Tsunami would be an appropriate name. And after he explained to the cowboys what the name means, they started using it, too.

"The redhead from Ireland is known as Moana," a name that needs no explanation. "Braids there is a Paiute indian whose hair says it all. And the last one is called Hillee because she has the biggest chest."

Despite Frederick's attempts to keep his thoughts as well as his actions professional during the examinations, he can't help mentally categorizing each of the "employees."

Mustang Maggie appears to be a take-charge, domineering exhibitionist who knows how to please but takes no crap.

Tsunami is teeny compared with the others but perfectly proportioned and probably plies her talent with a paucity of conversation.

Moana would be the palest were it not for the Contessa, and her playful smile suggests a mischievous nature.

As for Braids, she appears unpredictable, looks even more exotic than Tsunami and clearly is the most beautiful.

Hillee has a pretty face and a compliant nature, but her abundance of flesh is grudgingly surrendering itself to the unkind influence of gravity.

An hour and a half later, after completing the examinations while receiving a number of indelicately phrased offers of "companionship," Doc and Frederick depart, much to Frederick's relief.

"I didn't know how right I was when I accused you this morning of having a wicked streak, Doc. My God, what an experience."

"You'll get used to it, my boy," Doc winks. "And, by the way, don't expect any money for what you did today."

"Fine, Doc. If you don't want to share your fee, it's perfectly all right with me. But, out of curiosity, how much does the Contessa pay you?"

"Nothing. Not a cent," Doc says matter of factly.

"You do this out of the kindness of your heart, I suppose," Frederick replies sarcastically.

"No, for years after becoming a widower, I've used the barter system. I perform a service for them, and they reciprocate, although I don't think that's the word they'd use to describe our arrangement."

"The hell you say!" Frederick exclaims in genuine astonishment.

"Look, son, I may be old, but I'm not dead. Not yet anyway. And as long as all of my essential equipment is in working order, I'm going to stick to the same deal. And if you want to get 'paid,' you'll just have to do the same."

"Not likely, you old reprobate," Frederick laughs. "But just for the record, how much is the fee for each of the girls?"

"About three dollars, plus tips if the client feels generous," Doc explains.

"Is the Contessa still 'active'?" Frederick asks.

"Yep, but only a few of the wealthiest ranchers and businessmen in the state can afford her. You can, if you're willing to let go of five hundred dollars."

"Five hundred dollars! Are you serious?" Even the enormously wealthy Frederick considers that a small fortune for such a service.

"You see, Frederick, Contessa Bianca has become quite rich, and she knows how curious men are about what an experience would be like with her. Paying five hundred dollars to have sex with her is like purchasing a much-envied status symbol. After all, how many men can say they have gone to bed with a genuine albino?"

"Well, Doc," Frederick phews as they part to go to their separate offices, "I have to admit this is a day I'll never forget."

"Excellent," Doc beams. "That's what I intended when I put that note on your door."

Chapter Eight

Dr. Carlisle Opens His Office

Harvey Barrett, Agnes Pratt, and Lenora Ingram arrive early to make a good impression on their new employer when he walks into his waiting room at noon. Harvey, a retired New York City high school business teacher who appears to be a good twenty pounds underweight, moved west five years previously because of respiratory problems. He will serve as receptionist and bookkeeper. Agnes, a rotund widow in her early fifties with a reputation for being the best pie maker in the territory, will fill the cook-housekeeper position. And Lenora, an attractive young lady who recently completed medical training in San Francisco, will be the nurse and surgical assistant. She is a Wyandotte native eager to return to her hometown to rejoin her large number of relatives.

"Welcome, all of you," Frederick begins. "I am Dr. Frederick Carlisle, and I look forward to working with you. I think you will find I am not hard to get along with if you do your jobs well and with as little supervision as possible after we have gotten into a comfortable routine.

"I've written job descriptions, duties, and responsibilities for each of you. I'd like for you to study them carefully before you return tomorrow, at which time I'll meet with you individually to answer any questions you may have, as well as hear any suggestions you would like to make.

"I am always open to suggestions. I'm new to the West, and you are not. So I can always use guidance. I trust you will be equally open to suggestions and adjustments I think are necessary as I build my practice.

"I am informal by nature and prefer a pleasant working environment. And, finally, I have just one ironclad set of rules: We turn no one away; we treat every patient with equal respect regardless of his or her status in life or ability to pay; and we do everything humanly possible to promote good health for those who are curable and all we can to make the terminally ill as comfortable and as peaceful as possible.

"Any questions or comments?"

"Just one for now," Agnes says, rising to her feet and looking at the other two employees to make sure she isn't speaking out of place. "Can you make me a list of things you like to eat and things you don't?"

"Certainly, Agnes," Frederick smiles. "I'll have that ready for you tomorrow. Anyone else? No? Well, make yourselves at home. We open the office each day at eight o'clock and close at four, or as soon as we attend to our last patient.

"Oh, and we will close at noon this Wednesday. I have some personal business to attend to in the afternoon."

***

"How'd your first day go, Frederick," Doc inquires casually at their 7 p.m. dinner at the hotel.

"Fine. Good start, I'd say. My employees have strong credentials, and they seem pleasant enough."

"Well, my friend," Doc begins. "I know all three of them, and I can tell you the Van Sheltons did a good job recruiting them. Except for Lenora; I'll take credit for her hiring. I think you will be pleased with them all."

Shifting the subject to give Doc a little payback for the mischievous prank at the Gentlemen's Club, Frederick clears his throat loudly, leans closer to the older man and whispers: "Taken any 'payment' yet from our visit to the club this morning?"

"Hush your mouth, sir," Doc snaps. "I've told you all you're going to hear about that arrangement. So don't bother to ask again. And, by the way, my womanless colleague, have you satisfied any of your own needs with, say, Mustang Maggie or Tsumani? Bet you've never dangled your fishing line into any of those waters before, have you?"

"I'm a gentleman, Doc," Frederick goads. "And gentlemen never tell, do they?"

"Oh, horse shit, son. Just eat your meal and get a good night's sleep. If you don't have any patients after noon tomorrow, I'd like for you to ride out to the Turner place again with me. The time has come to level with the family on what kind of future Preston is likely to have."

"Done, Doc. I'd like to see Preston again. Bram thinks very highly of him. Figures his family and his friends are going to take the prognosis pretty hard."

The two physicians sit and talk casually over coffee for another hour before leaving for their homes. Frederick cannot resist getting in one parting dig.

"Good night, Doc, and, please, give my regards to Braids,"

"Good night, Frederick, and, please, kiss my ass."

Chapter Nine

A Visitor Cloaked in Darkness

Night has fallen by the time Frederick opens his unlocked front door, making him glad he lit a table lamp before going to dinner. He has no matches on him and does not yet know his way around the place well enough to keep from bumping into things.

As Frederick bends to pick up the lamp to light his way to bed, he is startled to hear a woman's voice softly say, "Hello, Dr. Gorgeous." It is the Contessa, sitting comfortably in the middle of the couch with one leg tucked beneath the other, her fashionable dress spread out over most of the seat. Frederick knows her identity before he looks. No one else calls him that name. But what in the world is she doing in his waiting area?

"Surprised, Doctor?"

"You might say that," is all Frederick can think to reply. "What brings you here at this hour, Contessa?"

"I came after dark because I don't want to chance bruising your precious reputation by walking into a room full of patients. Actually, I have two questions. One for Dr. Carlisle, and one for Dr. Gorgeous. Do you have time for me?"

"Of course," Frederick assures her. "Ask away."

"I want to know what the chances are of an albino woman having an albino baby if she is married to a normal man. Is it fifty-fifty? A certainty? I'm talking about my sister."

"Gosh, Contessa, I don't know enough to advise you at the moment. But I'll be glad to research it in my medical books. Or, if need be, I can write to one or more of my many contacts throughout the country and give you a reasonably accurate answer. Would that be all right?"

"Sure, Doctor. I'd really appreciate that. It means a lot to me. I purposely never had children myself because I did not want to subject another human to the ridicule and gawking I've gone through. But my sister wants to have her own baby so badly she's taking the risk. She's already four months pregnant."

"Well, it's settled then," Frederick said. "I'll get right on it. Now, what's the question you have for Dr. Gorgeous, as you seem to delight in calling me?"

"Just this," the Contessa whispers, standing gracefully and raising her fingers to the bottom of her throat. "How would you like to receive your payment tonight?" she offers while slowly unbuttoning her black blouse, revealing the whitest of bare skin underneath.

Before the stunned Frederick can reply, the Contessa takes him by the hand, smiles knowingly, and silently coaxes him up the staircase.

Chapter Ten

Preston Gets His Prognosis

Preston Turner is understandably depressed. His family's initial optimism that he would regain use of his lower body has gradually diminished. He looks desperately at the two doctors, praying for a few words of hope.

They have none to give.

"I won't sugarcoat the prognosis, folks," Doc begins. "If Preston's legs were going to improve, we should have seen some evidence of it by now. I'm sorry. Very sorry."

"Oh, Doc," Mrs. Turner pleads, "surely that's not so. He's only sixteen, and he's so strong. Can't you possibly be wrong?"

"Could be, but it's unlikely, Sadie," Doc replies. "I don't want to hold out false hope to Preston or any of the rest of you.

"However, there is some good news, although I certainly understand Preston and the rest of you may not get much immediate consolation from it.

"You see, Preston's injuries will have no influence on how long he can live. They won't affect his mind either. He'll be perfectly normal in all other ways. He can get around by himself in a wheelchair, and, with a little assistance, he can ride in buggies, coaches, and trains, traveling anywhere he wants to go."

For the first time, the Turners turn to Dr. Carlisle, seeking his opinion. "You're a big city doctor with a degree from an important university. We love Doc and trust his word, but can you or anybody else you know do anything more for Preston? Money's no problem. We can take him anywhere."

"I'm afraid not, Mrs. Turner," Frederick says compassionately. "There are doctors at our best schools doing research on injuries to the spine, but they haven't yet found the answers we're all hoping for. No one can say when, or even if, they ever will. I can only assure you they will never give up trying.

"But, Preston, I'd like to make one offer to you, if I may. Our mutual friend, Bram Van Shelton, tells me you are really smart and like to learn. So, I've talked to Bram's brother, Ruben, who has a big personal library. And I have a pretty good one myself. Anyway, my point is that our libraries are yours to use. And more than that, Ruben and his well-educated wife, Lillian, and I enjoy discussing books and would be very pleased to have you join us at our get-togethers."

Preston, who has said nothing since Doc and Frederick arrived, remains silent. But the tears streaming down his cheeks speak for him. He considers his life over.

***

"It's times like these that make being a doctor a hard thing," Doc sighs as he and Frederick ride back to town. Wonderful kid like that! It's a hard thing."

"Yeah, Doc. There's a universe of things we don't yet know. But what we do know is all we have to work with. We know enough to do a lot of good for a lot of patients. That's what has to keep us going.

"Preston will come around in time. He's not ready to accept this yet, but he can still run the ranch from a business standpoint. I'm going to speak with Harvey Barrett about tutoring Preston in accounting and other business methods when Preston's ready.

"I understand that even before the accident, Preston's dad intended all along for him to eventually take control of the ranch. Harvey can help give him the business background to do that well."

"Damn right, Frederick. There's a bunch of us who aren't about to give up on that boy."

Chapter Eleven

Trial Year Moves Rapidly Along

Dear Honoria,

You are indeed a remarkable woman. True to your word, you've written faithfully and often. No doubt we have stayed well informed on the happenings in each other's lives.

I've done the best I know how of describing to you this part of the country, its people, and its good and bad qualities.

But, somehow, that seems inadequate. I'm convinced you need to see it for yourself. So I am proposing you come to visit for at least two or three months, maybe longer. I cannot in good conscience marry you under any other circumstances. It just would not be fair to you.

As you know from my previous letters, I have become convinced I belong here. My practice is going well, and after a suspicious start, people are learning to like me as a person, and trust and respect me as a physician.

I would like for you to get to know the Van Sheltons, the Bodines, Doc, my employees, and some other friends and patients. I especially want you to get to know Lillian because some years ago she made the move I am asking you to consider. I suspect she knows from experience the answers to all the questions, doubts, and fears you may have.

If you are willing to come, I will make all necessary arrangements. The Van Sheltons are eager to have you as their guest during your stay. I hope you will say yes. Without sounding too dramatic, it's the only chance we have for a life together. We both have to be sure we are making a decision that will lead to happiness and not regret.

Lovingly, Frederick

Frederick and Honoria have kept their promise to write regularly, and their letters are candid and detailed. She continues her social life, she reports, including being escorted by several men to a variety of parties, dinners, the theater, and a few operas. She even tells him of an unexpected proposal of marriage she politely declined.

On his part, Frederick fully describes his friends, the community, his patients, and his medical practice. He gives her so much information on Doc, the Van Sheltons, and the Bodines she feels as if she already knows them.

Frederick even tells her about Doc taking him on that surprise visit to the Gentlemen's Club, and what the decor and "the girls" look like. He spares her the details of their "invitations" and their nicknames. And, of course, he makes no mention of the Contessa's visit to his home.

Nor does Frederick tell her about his meeting with Stephanie on that Wednesday afternoon soon after his arrival. The subject matter is both too personal and too professionally restrictive for any physician to discuss, even with a fiancé or a spouse.

Frederick was correct in thinking he detected some discomfort between Stephanie and Jesse. Amid some awkwardness and more than a few tears during their meeting, Stephanie tells Frederick she and Jesse are distressed by not having a single pregnancy in their three years of marriage. Both want children. Several, in fact.

"I've seen a specialist, Freddy," she revealed. "I haven't told Jesse yet, but on a shopping trip to San Francisco a couple of months before you moved here, I made the appointment. The doctor could find nothing wrong with me and suggested the problem might be Jesse's."

"Well, Stephanie, why haven't you shared this information with your husband? It does seem the logical next step."

"You're right about that, Freddy, except you must understand Jesse is a very proud man who has already had enough to challenge his self esteem. First, he was a poor man who married into a wealthy family, and second, he went in an instant from one of the most respected and feared men in the West to a man with a crippled gun hand. Now, to have him think he isn't 'man enough' to father a child . . . . Surely you can understand what that could do to him."

"Would you like for me, in my capacity as both a friend and a physician, to talk about this with Jesse?"

"Oh, goodness no! I mean, as much as I appreciate the offer, I don't think that would be wise for the time being."

"So, what do you propose to do, Stephanie? You can't go on indefinitely with this problem agitating your relationship."

"I know. I know, Freddy. I just wanted to talk with you about it for now. I think I'll give us another half year, and if I don't become pregnant by then, I'll tell Jesse about my seeing the specialist and find out if he is willing to talk with you. I know he won't talk with Doc. Jesse would be too embarrassed for that. He might be too embarrassed to talk with you. And I have no idea if he would be willing to seek medical advice from a stranger in San Francisco."

"Well, I'm here for you and Jesse anytime, Stephanie. You know that."

"Yes, I do. And thanks for listening. You're the only person I have the confidence to talk to about it."

***

"Telegram for you, Dr. Carlisle," Charlie Benson says as he hand-delivers the message in Frederick's office.

"A telegram?" Frederick reacts in surprise. "Well, thanks, Charlie," he says, retrieving some tip money from his pocket. Then, closing his office door for privacy, Frederick reads the following words:

> *So glad to receive your letter. Been hoping for invitation. Will inform you of anticipated arrival time.*
> *Love, Honoria*

Jubilant, Frederick rushes out of his office and into the waiting room, telegram in hand, and shouts "Yahoo!"

Simultaneously startled and amused, Lenora and Harvey interrupt their duties and stare, grinning in anticipation. "Gracious sakes, Dr. Carlisle," Lenora reproves mildly, "you sound like a cowboy who just wrestled a steer to the ground. What in the world's gotten into you?"

"Honoria's accepted my invitation to come for a visit," Frederick exclaims. "Honoria, my fiancé."

"Well, that's a relief, doctor," Harvey grins. "I thought for a second you were taking us unawares with some of that western lingo you've been attempting to adopt. Anyway, sir, very happy to hear the news. We'll all be glad to meet her."

Three of the four patients in the waiting room break into spontaneous applause, sharing Dr. Carlisle's happiness. The fourth patient, Greta Swensen, does not. Greta, a very pretty daughter of Swedish immigrants, is trolling for a husband, faking an illness to have some time alone with Dr. Carlisle.

She abandons her chair and leaves without a word.

"When's she coming, Doctor?" Lenora wants to know. "We need to be ready to give her the full Wyandotte welcome. And don't forget to keep Mrs. Pratt up to date. She will want to bake something extra special."

"Thank you all very much. Now, Harvey, send in my next patient," Frederick instructs, knowing his mind is so distracted he will have difficulty getting through the afternoon before riding to the Golden Eagle Ranch to share the good news with the Van Sheltons and the Bodines. And he is right. Time doesn't sprint; it crawls.

Chapter Twelve

The Contessa Gets Her Answer

True to his word, Fredrick researches, as the Contessa has requested, the chances of her albino sister having an albino baby even though she is married to a normal man. He sends word for the Contessa to visit either during or after office hours, whichever she prefers.

She chooses after hours and enters his waiting room a few minutes after his staff has left for the day. "Come in and have a seat," Frederick says cheerfully. "And, Contessa, I won't delay the news. It's good."

While the Contessa listens intently and patiently, Frederick explains in detail the variety of forms and consequences of albinism. As she nods in confirmation to several of the points he makes, Frederick realizes the Contessa is much more intelligent and informed than he has given her credit for.

"Here's what I found that will be of most interest to you. An albino whose mate is also an albino will likely have an albino baby. An albino whose mate is not an albino but who can be a carrier because of albinism in the family history, could produce an albino baby. But because you informed me that your sister's husband not only is normal but also has no family history of albinism, her baby has a very small chance of being an albino."

"Oh, thank God. I am so grateful, and I really appreciate your checking this out for me. I am so very relieved.

"I have one additional question for you," she suggests, smiling for the first time since entering his office. "I'm just itching to know—and you are aware I'm not the least bit shy about prying—if what I hear is true about a fiancé coming for a visit?"

"It's true," Frederick confirms. "Guess everybody in Wyandotte knows by now. I was so excited about her accepting my invitation I blurted it out to everyone in my office. Guess they've been doing a little blurting of their own."

"Well, I'm happy for you, my handsome friend. I sincerely hope everything works out for the two of you. 'Course, if it does, I suppose that means I'll have to start paying cash for my doctor bills," she teases.

Halfway through her exit to the outside, the Contessa turns slightly toward Frederick, gives him her naughtiest wink, and says, "'Course, if things don't work out . . . ."

Chapter Thirteen

Frederick's Acceptance Grows

Honoria's impending visit has a double-edged effect on Frederick's medical practice. On the negative side, there is an amusing drop-off in appointments made by healthy young women. On the positive side, his work with Doc Haggerty, especially in the many homes he visits with the highly respected doctor, gradually earns Frederick some trust in the area, resulting in more demand for his services.

Just as Mr. Van Shelton predicted when Frederick first arrived, people appreciate the improvement he has brought to their health and especially that of their children. They also respect Frederick and his staff for never embarrassing them over payment when they have none to give.

As for Frederick himself, he takes a measure of pride and pleasure advancing from "outsider" to "the doctor who talks funny." He also puts forth a commendable effort to fit in, attending local civic and church activities, weddings, and funerals.

Support grows from a variety of sources: the Van Sheltons, the Bodines, Frederick's staff, and, of course, Doc. Expressions of approval spread from Frederick's patients to their family members and friends. Even the Contessa and her girls put in a good word to their clients, especially the cowboys nursing a variety of injuries and ailments.

As time for Honoria's arrival nears, Frederick feels confident about the professional part of the life his intended will share if she agrees to move west permanently. He still worries about her being able to adapt to a much more limited social life with a much different group of people from those with whom she is accustomed to associating. Not to mention the absence of theaters, opera houses, luxurious stores in which to shop, and all other such advantages of big-city life.

Mrs. Van Shelton, with the enthusiastic support of Lillian and Stephanie, has already anticipated this potential stumbling block by making plans for a number of small gatherings to introduce Honoria to their friends, and they plan to top things off with a splendid dinner-dance near the end of Honoria's visit.

Even Bram, Frederick's roughneck friend, is making welcoming plans of his own. Bram detests social gatherings, but when Frederick tells him Honoria has a great love for horses and is a skilled rider, he makes it his business to shop around for the finest horse and saddle money can buy. He also lets it be known that although he won't attend the parties, he will be available to join Honoria on rides to show her how a large working ranch functions. Bram figures such knowledge will be an important part of her education about life so far away from New England.

Everyone seems to understand, without being either asked or told, the goal is to make sure Honoria receives a realistic knowledge of what her life would be like if she says yes to Frederick's one condition that they live in Nevada. Everyone will put his or her best foot forward, but there will be no attempt to sway Honoria against her will. She will be told and shown the truth.

With plans for Honoria's visit basically complete and his practice progressing satisfactorily, Frederick's hopes that all will turn out well increase. He and his staff have fallen into a comfortable working routine. Harvey, Agnes, and Lenora are all conscientious, reliable, pleasant, and need little supervision.

The only regret Frederick has since forsaking the lifestyle of his parents, grandparents, and great-grandparents is the cavern of loneliness even friends and life-saving work in the community cannot possibly fill.

Only a wife and children can. But now Honoria is coming, and she can make everything right. Surely, she will see why he belongs in Wyandotte, and how she can make a good life with him almost a continent away from Boston.

Things are looking promising.

Chapter Fourteen

Reality Panics Preston

The same cannot be said for Preston Turner.

Before his injury, Preston, a strongly built, energetic teenager with boyish good looks, was extremely excited that he was about to experience sex for the first time. Duggin Blankenship, the crusty old ranch foreman, promised to take Preston on the next cattle drive and treat him to the mysterious pleasures of a bordello when all the business was finished. Duggin's only stipulation was that Preston's mother never know. Preston readily agreed. Like most teenage boys, he would have agreed to anything short of death for the experience. He had been anticipating it for months.

Immediately after his accident, Preston's mind was occupied by two more pressing concerns: staying alive and finding out if he was going to be permanently paralyzed. Eventually, however, the already deeply depressed young man got around to cataloging all the other things being stomped by that horse would rob him of.

And then it hits him. Hits him so hard he breaks out in a cold sweat of panic. What about the sex he has never known? Is that gone, too?

"I have to know!" Preston screams. "I have to know right now!"

His shouts frighten his family, and they rush through his bedroom door to his side. "What is it, boy?" his father implores, bending over his distraught son. His mother takes his hands in hers, trying her best to calm him. His two younger siblings linger in the background, too scared to say anything.

"I have to see Dr. Carlisle," Preston demands. "As soon as you can get him out here. Please! No questions! Just get him out here now!"

"What about Doc Haggerty? Wouldn't you rather see him?" his mother insists.

"No. Listen to me. Only Dr. Carlisle."

"All right, son," his father replies. "I'll ride right to town and get him myself. "What do you want me to tell him? Are you in more pain? Has your condition changed?"

"No! No!! No!!! Tell him I just want to see him fast. I'm not in pain. I just have some things to ask him and him alone," pleads Preston, who is too embarrassed about the subject of sex to tell his father, let alone his mother, He wants Dr. Carlisle for two reasons. The doctor is young himself and will understand better than Doc how urgently important the matter is to him, and because he has a superior education at one of the nation's finest schools, Dr. Carlisle surely must know more.

Mr. Turner rides to town as fast as his swiftest horse can get him there. His concern is easy for Dr. Carlisle to read; it is written all over the anxious parent's face. And although Mr. Turner declares he has no idea what the source of Preston's urgent request is, Dr. Carlisle does. But he doesn't share his thought, silently cursing the topic he has been carefully avoiding and resenting its rising to the surface of Preston's consciousness.

Preston's deepening depression is Frederick's biggest concern now that the boy's life is out of danger and his ribs, cuts, and bruises have mostly healed. Frederick is prepared to have this talk with Preston, but he dreads it.

"What a hell of a talk to have to have with a sixteen-year-old boy just discovering what it is like to have romantic and sexual feelings for young women and eager to act on them," Frederick agonizes. "And I'm the one who has to tell him he might never get to know."

The ride to the Turner ranch ends too quickly as far as Frederick is concerned. He is consumed with apprehension, especially when Preston awkwardly and with painful embarrassment confirms his suspicions. The boy is blushing beet red and avoiding looking directly at him.

"Why me and not Doc, Preston?" Dr. Carlisle wants to know. "He's your primary doctor, and you've known him all your life. It's not that I'm not willing; it's just I'll have to give him a reason why I stepped in ahead of him on his patient."

"I don't mean any disrespect to Doc," Preston makes clear. "But because you're young and have a fiancé and will be starting a family, I think you'll understand better. So what can you tell me? I've got to know. I can't stand not knowing, so, please, Dr. Carlisle, be truthful and frank with me."

"All right, Preston. I'll tell you everything I know. But you must understand there are no certain answers. There are many, many possibilities. Let's start with the positive ones.

"Because you are a paraplegic, and not a quadriplegic—conditions Doc and I have explained before—you stand a better chance of being able to have sex. It's not certain, and mostly it depends on how your body responds to the injury.

"Without being too technical, there are two main ways a male becomes aroused enough for sex. One is through the mind, seeing someone who physically excites him or thinking sexual thoughts about a woman. The other is through touch or tactile stimulation.

"Many paraplegics are capable of being aroused, and those who are, usually are capable of having some degree of sexual activity. Experimentation with a willing and sympathetic partner is the best way to make those discoveries. Keep in mind, Preston, there is much more to sex than intercourse itself. A person's mind is very much involved. Sexual function and pleasure are mostly psychological."

"And the negative, Dr. Carlisle?" Preston asks with obvious trepidation.

"Mainly, it's that although some paraplegics may be capable of reaching a climax—that is, having an orgasm—I can't promise you that you will be able to feel it physically."

"How will I know? When will I know?"

"You will know by checking to see what happens when you think sexual thoughts. You can check for yourself. But be patient. Nothing is likely to happen if you try to force it while you're worried or anxious.

"I know you don't want to hear me say let's wait and see what happens. But that's what we have to do. And, remember, Preston, I'll talk about this anytime you want.

"Now, because you are the patient, you will have to let me know what I can say to your parents. We will have to tell them something. I can't leave the house with them worried to death. And you know I have to tell Doc. But he is bound by the same doctor-patient confidentiality I am."

"Gosh, Dr. Carlisle, I wish we didn't have to tell my folks anything. We've never ever talked about such things. Just tell them I had some questions about my chances of getting married and having a family, and make it clear you told me everything I need to know and for them not to mention it to me. OK?"

"Right. I'll do as you say, Preston. And if you need me, just send word."

"Thanks, doctor. I had to have some hope."

Chapter Fifteen

Honoria Travels to Wyandotte

After eight months in Wyandotte, Frederick is adjusting better to some of the changes in his lifestyle. Especially doing for himself a few of the many tasks, small and large, previously handled by people in service at his Boston estate. Nothing as menial as washing and ironing clothes or occasionally cleaning his living or working quarters, or caring for his horse and buggy. Between Mrs. Pratt, the nearby Chinese laundry, and the local stable, all of those needs are being cared for with little oversight necessary.

However, he is occasionally preparing a late snack for himself when he returns home from house calls long after Mrs. Pratt has left for the day. He also has learned to make a passable cup of coffee, and he is fetching and heating water for bathing. He has no time and no appreciative guests for the gourmet meals he enjoyed making in Boston.

He often wonders how, or if, Honoria would adjust to doing similar chores both for him and for herself. "Good question," he allows before dropping such an unpleasant thought that need not be dealt with until the time comes. Frederick's practice keeps him busy, but how would Honoria while her time away?

That answer will be coming soon, he realizes, because he is holding in his hand a telegram with the news of Honoria's scheduled arrival in five days. Frederick and his supportive friends and employees will need to get busy completing preparations.

Surprisingly, the person who anticipates where assistance is most immediately needed is Bram, of all people. The family misfit is thinking ahead of everyone else, and he lets Frederick know straight away.

"For a doctor with a fancy-ass degree from a snotty college, you are sometimes dumber than steer shit, Freddy," Bram fusses as he marches without notice or invitation into his friend's office ahead of several patients awaiting their turn.

"Would it inconvenience you, Bram, if I shut the door before you say whatever it is you think can't wait until I'm free?"

"It's about your crazy idea of riding fifty miles alone to the railway station to protect Honoria on her stagecoach trip to Wyandotte. First, you'd probably get lost. Second, you'd likely shoot yourself in the foot drawing a pistol against anyone trying to rob the stage.

"So, forget about it. I'm goin' in your place. I'm much better suited for the job than you, no question about that. So that's the end of it. Don't waste my time with any of your educated bullshit.

"I know what yer thinkin', Freddy. Don't worry," Bram reassures as he heads out the door, pausing only long enough to say, "I'll make certain Honoria knows no one else in this family is as crude and unsophisticated as me."

***

If Bram had not been holding a sign with "Honoria" written on it, he never would have located her on his own. The woman who departs the train and approaches him, introduces herself and extends her hand looks absolutely nothing like the beautiful young visitor he is expecting. Her face is masked by a veil hanging from a frumpy-looking hat, and her baggy ankle-length dress is the color of mud. Black gloves hide the age of her hands, and her lace-up shoes look as if they belong to someone's great-granny.

"Nice disguise," Bram compliments with a broad smile. "If you hadn't identified yourself, I wouldn't have suspected." He is familiar

121

enough with scoundrels and lowlife characters to perceive that Honoria has painstakingly made herself unattractive to ward off the unwanted attention a pretty young woman traveling alone would otherwise receive.

"Thanks, Bram. So glad you approve," Honoria laughs in a voice at least thirty years younger than her outfit indicates. It is a nice voice, friendly and unassuming, Bram surmises, perhaps unaware he is already being charmed by an intelligent woman with subtle qualities conspicuously absent in the females of his acquaintance.

As Honoria hooks her arm around his while they walk away from the train station, she asks: "Think I'll have any place along the way to reassemble myself before I see Frederick or meet any more members of your family? I'd probably frighten the children in this getup, not to mention causing your parents to question Frederick's taste in Eastern women."

Bram laughs at her concession to vanity. "We'll be making our last way station stop about twenty miles short of Wyandotte. You can change there. Have to admit, I'm kinda hankerin' to see what you look like myself."

"Well, don't set your expectations too high, Bram. I wouldn't want to disappoint you."

"Guess we'll just have to wait and see," Bram winks.

"Guess we will, Bram," Honoria teases.

***

After Bram gets Honoria situated in the hotel, he heads to the nearest saloon. He has three hours to do a little drinking and relaxing before meeting her for dinner in the hotel restaurant. Uncharacteristically, Bram restricts his whiskey intake out of respect for Honoria and his friend Frederick. He insisted on bringing her safely to Wyandotte on the stagecoach, and he intends to do just that.

Honoria orders a small steak, well done, and a salad. Bram has the same, except much bigger, rare, with a side of fried potatoes. As they are both hungry, they eat a while in silence.

When Bram can delay talking no longer, he chooses a topic he knows well—horses. "Freddy tells me you like horses and enjoy riding," he says, watching as Honoria finishes the last bite of her meal.

"I do, Bram. Actually, it's more than a liking. I love horses. Always have, since I was a child. I think they are among God's greatest gifts to humankind. They are strong, beautiful and willing companions when they are treated with kindness and respect.

"You know what I like best, Bram? I feel somehow free from the cares of the world when I'm out riding in the countryside of New England. I know you've been around them all your life, both working horses and those you ride for pleasure, I presume?"

"Yeah, I prefer mustangs for working. They are smaller than some other horses, but they are sturdy and tough. In case you don't know, mustangs are wild horses, descendants of the tame animals Spaniards introduced to this country centuries ago. You'll get a chance to ride one, if you like."

"I'd love it, Bram. I hope to do a lot of riding while I'm visiting, and because I've been told you know the most about working the ranch, I hope you'll have time to show me around. I'd like to get a feel for how people work with cattle on these huge spreads—if that's the right word?"

"I've already volunteered for that pleasure, Honoria, and so has Jesse. Your timing is good, too, because we don't have any cattle drive scheduled for quite some time. Between me and Jesse, we'll show you everything you want to see."

"Great, Bram. I'm eager for the experience."

"Well, fine. I also have something waiting for you at the Golden Eagle."

"What is it, Bram?"

"Can't say. Wouldn't be a surprise if I did."

***

Bram and Honoria board the stage leaving at daybreak so the driver can cover thirty of the fifty miles to Wyandotte before sundown. The overnight accommodations will be primitive but clean at the way station, and arrival in Wyandotte is expected by early afternoon the following day.

Two other passengers, both men, join them for the trip. One is a fiftyish, well-dressed salesman whose eventual destination is California, after a couple of business stops along the way. He tips his hat to Honoria, introduces himself as Raymond Crayford, and shakes hands with both Bram and Honoria. The other rider is quite a contrast but just as polite. "Call me Russ," he says, taking off his faded hat and nodding in deference to Honoria.

Russ doesn't shake hands, and the three other passengers are grateful. The old-timer's shabby clothing looks as if it has never been introduced to soap and water. His well-worn boots are covered in grime, and Russ smells like an abandoned outhouse.

From their departure until the stage reaches its first stop to change horses, Honoria gags every time Russ lifts his bottom off the seat to switch into a more comfortable position. She is exceedingly grateful he has decided to ride on the exterior when they resume their journey, unaware that Bram took Russ aside during the stop, explained as respectfully as he could that Russ was "smelling a bit ripe," and paid him three times the cost of the trip to ride on top the rest of the way.

Having more pleasant air to breathe helps Honoria endure the final leg of the bumpy ride to Wyandotte, where she arrives looking every bit the twenty-three-year-old she is after shedding her matronly disguise that morning. Bram, the driver, his shotgun partner, Raymond, and Russ are mightily impressed, to say the least.

Bram observes a healthy-looking woman about five-foot three-inches tall with the trim, fit body of an athlete. If there is an excess ounce of weight anywhere on her, it is doing an excellent job of hiding. Her hair is an ordinary brown color, but it is extraordinarily thick and naturally wavy. Her face is pretty, not beautiful, and her eyes are striking. They may be hazel, Bram reckons, because they look brown but contain sparkling flecks of green and gold. Her hands are small, but not delicate. Like the rest of her, they look strong. And above all else, Bram, being a man's man, values her self-assurance.

"Hell of a woman," Bram concludes. "Freddy is one lucky son of a bitch!"

Chapter Sixteen

Frederick is a No-Show

Bram helps Honoria step from the stagecoach, and she searches eagerly for Frederick. He is not there. She looks questioningly at Bram, who shrugs his shoulders in puzzlement. But he soon sees the explanation headed their way.

Deputy Sheriff Aaron Brinkley nods at Bram, tips his hat to Honoria and says, "Ma'am, Bram. Dr. Carlisle asked me to meet you and let you know he regrets he can't have lunch with you. Seems Mrs. Pinrod's baby decided to come this morning and there's complications. So he expects to be at her place about five miles outside of town for quite some time. He's plumb sorry, Miss Honoria; he was all dressed up and slicked out to greet you."

"Thank you kindly, Mr., uh –"

"The name's Aaron Brinkley, ma'am. I'm the deputy sheriff, and I'm happy to do anything I can for Dr. Carlisle, and anything I can do for you while you're visitin'."

Honoria turns to Bram, punches him good-naturedly on the shoulder, and says, "Well, guess your saloon's going to have to wait. Appears you're stuck with me for lunch as well as the buggy ride to the ranch. I'm disappointed Frederick couldn't be here, especially because I got all dressed for the occasion. But right now, I'm famished. So where are you taking me?"

"Best place is the hotel restaurant, Honoria. And I think you'll be surprised how good the food is."

"Sounds good. You'll find I'm not one of those females with a delicate appetite, so a good meal will make the trip to the ranch much more enjoyable."

***

The buggy ride is only slightly less uncomfortable than the stagecoach, and with her appetite satisfied, all Honoria can think of is a long hot bath to relieve the aches and pains emanating, it seems, from every pore in her body. She keeps these thoughts to herself, though. Wouldn't want to give Bram the impression she is a pampered old softy Easterner, if he doesn't think that already.

"Almost there," Honoria. "Just a couple of more miles."

"Good, Bram. Seems like an eternity since I left Boston. I'll be glad to stay put in one place for a while. Now, tell me, honestly, do I look reasonably presentable to meet your family?"

Raising an eyebrow and moving his head up and down and side to side in an exaggerated inspection, Bram mutters, "Reckon you'll do." What he wanted to say was, "If you looked any better, somebody would have to hog-tie me!"

Like Frederick, Honoria is accustomed to luxury, but she is nevertheless impressed with the rustic beauty of the Golden Eagle Ranch as it comes into view. The town is not to her liking, and neither is the ten miles of land between the hotel and the ranch. She feels so isolated seeing no houses or people along the way, although she is thankful they don't encounter a bear or a mountain lion or any other creature she conjures up in her imagination.

However, as she was informed by Frederick's detailed letters, the family is wonderful. They all turn out to greet her before she can enter the mansion.

"Welcome, my dear, welcome," Mr. Van Shelton smiles, taking Honoria's right hand in his and patting it enthusiastically with his left.

"So glad you are finally here," Mrs. Van Shelton says with a hug considerably gentler than her husband's handshake. "Allow me to introduce the rest of the family: My daughter, Stephanie, and her husband, Jesse, and my son Ruben, his wife, Lillian, and their children, Jonathan and Esther.

"Now, come into the house where we can make you more comfortable."

Honoria takes an immediate liking to them and appreciates that they have anticipated how tired she would be by planning a brief evening after dinner so she can bathe and get to bed early. Tomorrow will be a big day with a welcoming dinner and the presence of Frederick. She sleeps until noon.

Dinner is planned to the minutest detail. Mrs. Van Shelton, Stephanie, and Lillian want Honoria's first big event with the family and Frederick to be as nearly perfect as possible. The dining room is beautifully prepared but not formal. Dress is church-suitable—coats and ties for the men and dresses for the women. Tuxedos and gowns are being reserved for the extravagant dinner-dance party scheduled near the end of Honoria's stay. The menu includes beef, pork, and fish with all the trimmings—something to fit the tastes of everyone. The desserts, prepared by the family's proud kitchen staff, are heavenly.

The family gathers at six o'clock in the magnificent drawing room for drinks before dinner. Everyone is present: Mr. and Mrs. Van Shelton, Jesse, and Stephanie, Ruben and Lillian and their children. Shockingly, even Bram is attending—in a coat and tie no less. His parents are baffled, but Lillian and Stephanie are not. By the way he keeps hanging around Honoria, the women recognize his motives. Besides, he hasn't stopped talking about the way she handled herself on the trip. There's nothing subtle about his admiration.

Everyone is present. Everyone, that is, except Frederick. He is not long overdue, but enough to be annoying. Dinner cannot be delayed too much more without diminishing its quality, Mrs. Van Shelton worries. And too much time and effort have been expended to allow that to happen.

"Wonder what's keeping Freddy?" Mrs. Van Shelton asks. "He's been looking forward to this get-together so eagerly."

"Probably some patient showing up at closing time," Jesse suggests. "Hope Doc's near by so Freddy can get here before the food gets cold."

Even Mr. Van Shelton is concerned. He doesn't want the women to be disappointed. He and Ruben have done little to help, but he is aware of what has gone into the preparations and admires the women's efforts.

A half hour later, the family can wait no longer. They move to the dining room to enjoy the excellent meal, each somewhat nervous about Frederick's unexplained absence. Nevertheless, enjoyable conversation abounds, everyone eager to hear Honoria's impressions of the West.

Lillian and Stephanie inquire about the latest big–city fashions, and Jonathan and Esther relate their summer experiences in New England. Bram is eager to know whether early the next morning is too soon for Honoria's first ride to various parts of the ranch. He also reminds her she has a surprise coming, holding her in suspense.

As for Frederick, he is a no-show, and the reason is presumed by all to be a medical emergency.

They have no idea how right they are.

Chapter Seventeen

Tragedy Strikes

Frederick brings the news when he arrives at the ranch an hour after sunup the following day. Montgomery Turner, Preston's thirty-seven-year-old father, is dead. Worse, he was killed accidentally by a gunshot while wrestling a pistol out of his son's hands to stop him from committing suicide.

Mrs. Turner is an emotional wreck, the two younger children are traumatized, and Preston has closed tightly within himself, refusing to speak. He has not shed a single tear, just gazes aimlessly, rarely blinking his eyes, his stare seemingly frozen in one direction.

Shock is setting in as word spreads throughout the community, for the Turners are held in high esteem, far too good a family to be struck by accidents that paralyze a son and kill a father. And, as always, there is no rational answer to the question of "Why?"—an imploration to God since time immemorial after countless other seemingly senseless tragedies.

"Doc and I were called to the Turner ranch too late for me to send word I would miss last night's dinner," Frederick informs the family. "I am terribly sorry and apologize most sincerely to all of you, but especially to you, Honoria. I deeply regret our first meeting in Wyandotte is under such unfortunate circumstances."

"We all understand, son," Mr. Van Shelton assures Frederick.

"Yes, Frederick," Honoria adds. "You had no choice. I'm just sorry you and Dr. Haggerty were not able to save Mr. Turner. "

"No, he lived for a time after the accident, but he was dead when Doc and I got there. There was nothing we could do for Mr. Turner, but, folks, that family needs all the help we can give them right now. Mrs. Turner is in no shape to plan a funeral. Preston is in a trance for I do not know how long, and the other two children, Charles and Pamela, are in bad need of comforting and reassurance."

"Well," I have some suggestions," Mrs. Van Shelton interjects, taking charge of the situation. "Vincent and I can make arrangements at the funeral home, as well as for the wake and the church service. I know the Turners have their own cemetery on their property."

"Jesse and me'll see to preparing and closing the grave," Bram offers.

"I'll make a temporary marker until a more proper headstone can be ordered," Jesse volunteers.

"And Stephanie and I will bring those poor children here until their mother recovers enough to care for them," Lillian says, knowing their being with Jonathan and Esther will comfort and distract them more than any adults can.

"Good," Mr. Van Shelton says. "That seems to take care of everyone except Mrs. Turner and Preston. I presume, Frederick, that Preston has to be constantly monitored to keep him from trying again to do away with himself?"

"Mrs. Turner fortunately has two sisters nearby. They are with her now. Preston is being watched by their ranch foreman, Duggin Blankenship. Doc says those two have a close bond, and Duggin can be trusted to take care of him.

"But that's only a short-term solution. Doc plans to have a frank, tough talk with Preston after the funeral. We need to set him on the right path of responsibility, and we'll need to form a supervisory group with all of you men. But we can discuss that after the service."

"All right, everybody," Mrs. Van Shelton says, sensing the time has come to move on. "Let's join hands and have a prayer for the Turner family and then gather in the dining room for a meal. What has happened is just terrible, but we need the nourishment, as well as more pleasant conversation before we get about the business we discussed.

"Not to mention that Freddy and Honoria need some time for themselves. Lord sakes, she's been here more than two days, and they've hardly had a chance to say a dozen words to each other."

***

Doc waits one week after the funeral to gather his forces and attempt to break through to Preston before the young man becomes a hopeless case. Preston still is not speaking. He is barely eating, and he is plaguing his family with worry instead of providing the strength and leadership they desperately need.

"I'm fed up," Doc tells Frederick, Mr. Van Shelton, Jesse, and Bram before they enter the Turner house. Preston will be alone, except for his faithful caretaker, Duggin. Doc has warned them all, including Duggin, his tactics will be tough, and may even seem cruel.

"You'll just have to trust me, men," Doc insists. "All my experience as a doctor informs me we will be dead wrong in handling Preston as a kid, heaping our sympathy upon him, and excusing the way he is acting, accepting it as a normal reaction to all he is suffering.

"So bear with me, no matter what I say or do. Time will soon tell whether I'm right or wrong. And if I'm wrong, I'll admit it and get out of the way. But, make no mistake about it, a hell of a lot is at stake here, not only for Preston but also his entire family."

As they enter the house, Preston, seated in his wheelchair, is staring straight ahead, seeing nothing. Duggin is drinking coffee. Social niceties are bypassed; no one utters a greeting. The men approach Preston as a group with Doc a couple of steps in the lead.

Doc stops less than two feet from Preston's face, clears his throat noisily but fails to get Preston's attention. "Preston," Doc says loudly, "look at me. I'm here accompanied by the best friends you've got in this world, whether you know it or not."

Preston gives no reaction. Doc might as well be speaking to a rock.

"Preston," Doc tries again, "this won't take long. Give me your attention for just a few minutes."

Again, no reaction from Preston.

Doc steps within one foot of Preston's face, looks directly into the young man's eyes. He means business. "I will be heard, and you will pay attention."

Preston stares straight ahead. No reaction whatsoever.

Doc lifts his right arm, but not in a gesture. He slaps Preston's face so hard the wheelchair rocks sideways. Preston is shocked, hurt, and damned angry—the reaction Doc intended.

"What the hell, Doc?" Preston screams, shaking with fury. "You have no right to treat me this way. I didn't ask you or any of the rest of them to come here tonight. Get out of my house and take them with you!"

"Like hell I will," Doc shouts back. "I delivered you into this world, same as I did your parents. I've known you every day of your life. I've pulled you through measles, mumps, whooping cough, and a broken arm before that horse stomped you. I've earned the right to speak.

"So here it is with no crap attached. You've been dealt a bad hand; nobody's denying that. You're a paraplegic, and when you tried to kill yourself, it was your dad who died instead. And although you didn't mean for that to happen, it did. Nothing can be done about that, and you are partly responsible. You'll just have to live with it.

"Now, you're only sixteen, but the day your dad died struggling to save you, you forfeited the remainder of your childhood. You're a man now; you have to be. Someone has to run this ranch and look after your mother and your brother and sister. That someone is you. There is no one else.

"You see these men with me? They're here to make certain you know you are not alone. Mr. Van Shelton and Ruben are going to be your business counselors, helping you with all major decisions until you are of legal age to take control yourself. Your mother will have to sign all papers until then, and she has already agreed to do that.

"Bram, Jesse, and Duggin know everything there is to know about cattle and horses and running the working part of a ranch. They'll take care of that for the next couple of years.

"Dr. Carlisle and I will work with you medically, getting you to the point where you are doing everything possible physically. You're capable of a great deal more than you suspect.

"That's the way it is, Preston. You have a choice. Shape up and take your rightful place in this family and in this community, or go ahead and kill yourself, either fast with a gun or slowly as you've been doing since the accident that killed Montgomery.

"We'll give you two days to come around. Then we will be back with your mother and your siblings. We'll come through that front door and find you either dead or grown up and ready to act like a man.

"You have anything you want to say before we leave?"

Preston, his face and voice completely devoid of emotion or expression, says nothing.

Chapter Eighteen

Honoria Tries to Fit In

Honoria is thrilled with Bram's gift. She considers the elaborately detailed saddle a work of art, and she is mesmerized by the sight of the magnificent horse.

"Oh, Dear God," she whispers reverently as she beholds a champagne-colored palomino with a white mane, socks, tail, and broad blaze from the top of his head to the bottom of his nose. "Bram, you bought him for me? He is so conspicuously handsome, he's downright ostentatious. I love him!"

"Jesse helped me pick him out, so I have to give him a little credit, too."

"What's his name?" Honoria asks.

"That's up to you. Call him whatever you like."

"Hmm, let's see. He looks like royalty to me, so I think I'll call him Baron or Duke. No, no—I've got it, Bram. He deserves a higher rank than that. Let's dub him Crown Prince."

"Well, he'll have the most highfalutin name of any horse on the ranch, but if that suits you, it tickles me plumb to death. Now are you ready to take him for a ride?"

"You bet. Let's go!"

Jock, the stable hand who saddled the horses and brought them to Bram and Honoria, leans on the gate and watches enviously as the pair head to the range. "There goes a rich man out to spend the day with a pretty, rich woman, and here I am shoveling shit for thirty dollars a month and keep. Man, wished I'da been born a Van Shelton!"

***

Honoria loves being in the saddle. She rides, as she always has, astride the horse, much to the dismay of her father who gave up long ago trying to get her to "act like a lady and sit sidesaddle." She likes the control she has with a leg on each side of the animal, and she immediately feels the radiating power of this majestic twelve-hundred-fifty-pound stallion.

"Where are you taking me, Bram? Are we going to circle the ranch?'

"Not quite, Honoria," Bram smiles at her underestimation of the size of Western spreads. "It would take us a week to cover our land. I think we'll ride first to that high ridge yonder," Bram says, pointing to a spot about five miles away. Then we'll take a trail through the pine trees to a lake about five more miles away. Beautiful spot with a good view in every direction. We'll look around a bit and let the horses rest.

"By then we should be good and hungry, so we'll catch up with the ranch hands branding calves. Don't supposed you've ever eaten chuck wagon food?"

"Well, Bram, considering I've never even seen a chuck wagon, I think I can safely say I haven't. But I'm willing. Describe it to me."

"I told Cookie to prepare a typical meal today, so you could get an authentic feel for what eatin' on the range is like. So we're havin' beef stew, biscuits, and apple pie. I promise it's better than you're used to because it's all cooked outside. Might even have a little dirt in it for flavorin'."

Honoria laughs loudly. "Don't suppose a little western soil will cause any harm. Besides, I've worked up an appetite."

Bram's admiration grows by the hour for this woman. She may look small, but he's finding out she's tough, adventurous, and a damn good sport.

"Hell of a woman," he says to himself in words that are high praise coming from him.

***

"This food is absolutely delicious," Honoria exclaims. "Cookie, you've done yourself proud!" Not used to compliments from the men who continually rib him about the food, Cookie all but blushes at her praise.

Noticing the ranch hands are keeping their distance from her, Honoria is determined to soften their obvious impression of her as a rich, high-class Eastern beauty. "Don't be shy, boys," she teases charmingly. "Come on over and talk to me. Tell me how strong I look and how pretty my horse is," she jokes.

The men gather closer to Honoria but still mind their manners, aware that Bram is watching and listening sharply to make sure they observe his temporary ban on their swearing, bawdy jokes, and tobacco spitting.

Bram purposely has brought along no chairs, no table, and certainly no tablecloth or napkins. Everyone sits on the ground or on logs, eats out of tin plates, and uses cheap metal utensils. Honoria is getting the real treatment. The men appreciate her efforts to fit in and warm up to her questions about roping, branding, and living out in the elements for weeks at a time.

Near the end of the meal, Rufus Meade, the wiry, little longtime foreman, breaks out his harmonica. He is joined by a quartet of other rugged-looking men wearing dust-covered clothes, large hats, chaps, and spurs. As they gather in front of Honoria and Bram, they begin to harmonize "Red River Valley."

Honoria is both delighted and honored. She is taken aback by the unexpectedly handsome sounds emerging from these disheveled, sunbaked veterans of the range. She feels Bram's eyes lock on her when the lyrics express how much he will miss her "bright eyes and sweet smile" when she's gone.

When the men go back to work and she and Bram must outride the darkness heading home, Honoria feels a pang of regret that an end must come to what for her has been a unique experience.

As if to read her thoughts, Bram assures her there will be several more similar experiences with him and Jesse before her time in Nevada is up.

"I can tell you had a good time, Honoria. That pleasures me right considerable."

"Thank you, Bram. I'll remember this day."

Chapter Nineteen

Honoria Surprises Jesse

Honoria surprises Jesse with a request he doesn't see coming when he shows up at the stables to take his turn at an early morning ride with Frederick's bride to be.

"You want me to teach you how to shoot a gun?!"

"Yes, Jesse, if you're willing."

"But why me, Honoria. I'm sure Bram or Rufus Meade or any number of the other ranch hands would be glad to accommodate you."

"Well, I'll tell you why I want you to do it, Jesse. You've been around Stephanie and Lillian long enough to be used to aggressive women who don't fit the usual mold, so I'll be as frank as they are. If I'm stepping over the line of propriety, please tell me and I'll drop it.

"I want you to teach me because your reputation tells me you are the best. I'm intrigued by your past as a gunfighter, and I'd love to talk about it, if you will allow me."

"I declare, Honoria, the younger women of this household are forever taking me unawares. I sure didn't meet any like you where I come from. But, all right, give me a few minutes to collect some weapons and ammo, and we'll see how all this works out."

They ride for a while in silence, each enjoying watching the sun rise through the mist and slight fog following the previous night's rain. The chill is bracing, clearing their minds and leaving their everyday cares and concerns behind at the mansion. Their grand horses are fresh, full of energy, and eager to break into a vigorous run.

"By the way, Jesse, I want to thank you again for your part in selecting Crown Prince for me. I love him so much, I sometimes go to the stable just to look at him and run my hands over him. Your Patches is the only other horse on the Golden Eagle Ranch I'd compare him with. They're both so gorgeous. Don't know whether you think of horses as beautiful, but there's no denying these two are."

"No, I agree with you, Honoria. Beauty's not the main thing I look for in a horse, although it's one factor for me for my personal ride. But as far as a working horse is concerned, I don't care if it's uglier than a mud rail fence if it's good at its job.

"You know, I've had Patches since he was a colt. Trained him myself, so he knows me. Knows what to expect from me, and I have the same confidence in him. Means a lot to me, that horse does. More than most people do. Wouldn't part with him for anything.

"Now, why do you want to learn how to shoot a gun? Know anything about it?"

"Nothing. Fact is, I've never fired any weapon. But if I marry Frederick, I'll be spending a lot of time alone in our house, especially when he'll be gone all night doing something patients can't put off until morning.

"You may not believe this, Jesse, but I've never been alone in a house before. Even when my parents and siblings were not at home, we always had a staff of people to protect me. So, I don't know whether I'll be scared here or not, but it makes sense that I'll be less scared if I know how to protect myself."

"Good reasoning and you're right about that. I can show you the basics, if you're sure Frederick won't mind me not squaring it with him first."

"He won't have any objections. Fact is, he doesn't know much more than I do. I know his father took him hunting a few times when he was young, but he didn't like shooting animals and begged off years ago. I might end up having to teach him a thing or two."

"OK, but first let's allow these horses to run a few more miles, and then I have a good spot in mind to start our lessons. And I say lessons, Honoria, because it will take several to do this right and make sure you learn as much about gun safety as shooting. Sound all right with you?"

"Sure, I'm loving the ride anyway."

***

On the third of their dawn rides and shooting lessons, Honoria feels comfortable enough with Jesse to chance prying into the gunfighter part of his past she is so curious about. She doesn't know quite where to start, so she tells him how she's spent considerable time staring at him and wondering how it all can be true.

"Jesse, after I had been at the ranch enough time to get to know each of you individually, I found myself looking at you and your gun hand and trying to imagine how this seemingly mild-mannered, polite man who avoids being the center of attention could possibly have once been a gunfighter named J.D. Rohr, the kind they write about in those 'Dime Novels' back East."

"Oh, I don't think anybody ever wrote about me, Honoria."

"Perhaps, not. But they could have. I mean, I look at you and it boggles my mind to realize you have actually killed at least eight men that I know of—six in one-on-one gunfights and two others when you and Bram and your men caught up with those rustlers.

"It must take unbelievable courage to do that?"

"No, not really, Honoria. At least not in my case. Given a choice, I would have lived out my life without killing or even harming another living soul. But when I took the job as deputy in Big View, Colorado, I knew the time might come when I'd have to use my gun."

"Jesse, I have a big question I've been working myself up to asking, and it's not only very personal but a direct invasion of your innermost privacy. May I ask it without offending you? I promise I'll drop it immediately if you say so."

"Guess so. Go ahead. Ask."

"What does it feel like to kill somebody? To end somebody's life? Does it haunt you, or is it something a man learns to live with, especially in the West where there are so many challenges to life?"

"Whew. Hold on there just a second, Honoria. That one hit me right in the gut. Do you realize you're the only person who's ever asked me that? I mean, other than myself. But, it even surprises me that I'd like to answer your question. Doing so may—what's the right word—be healthy for me? You're educated, Honoria. What is it I'm trying to say?"

"Therapeutic, I think. It means good for the mind or a healing process."

"Yeah, that's purely what I mean. Well, the barefaced truth is killing someone, especially one-on-one, can be a mix of feelings. It can be sickening and full of guilt, or it can make you want to strut like a peacock. I should be ashamed to admit it, but part of me liked being admired and feared, having the reputation of being so fast with a gun that nobody had ever bested me.

"Truth is, I'm haunted by only one shooting. The first bothered me some simply because it was the first. I shot an outlaw named Angel Dutch Hendriks when I came upon him breaking into a store while I was a deputy making my rounds of the town one night. But I got over that in a hurry, and it doesn't bother me in the least now because I actually saved lives by taking his. He was a killer who favored hiding somewhere safe and shooting people in the back—and he wasn't particular about whether they were men, women or children if he had his reason for doing it.

"Four of the other five men I had gunfights with gave me no choice. I tried to talk each one out of it. I gave them a chance to back out without losing face, but they wanted the reputation they thought killing me would bring them. So I had to draw against them.

"Only one still bothers me, and I'll never get over it. I still have nightmares about it. Probably always will. He was no more than a boy, maybe sixteen. Cocky, arrogant. So certain he couldn't be beat."

"Well, Jesse, why didn't you just shoot him in his gun hand? Shake him up so much he'd realize how close he'd come to being killed?"

"Honoria, that question shows you must have read at least one of those silly novels. That's the only place you'll hear about somebody winning a gunfight by shooting the other man in his gun hand while he's drawing his pistol as fast as he can to kill you. Believe me when I tell you everybody always aims for the biggest target—the middle of the chest. Otherwise, you end up very dead yourself."

"And this death bothers you because he was just a kid?"

"Mostly. But the hell of it is, he lived for a minute or two after I shot him. I wish to God I'd walked out of the room, but I went up to him, and saw him lying on his back pleading with his eyes and reaching both arms up toward me. He couldn't talk, but it was clear he was begging me to return the bullet to its chamber and, somehow, give him back his life. And that's the way he died, knowing too late the mortal mistake he made trying to be a gunfighter.

"Honoria, losing these two fingers is the only thing that's saved me from that boy's fate. As sure as the sun rises, sooner or later someone would have outdrawn me. I'd be dead instead of living the good life I have with Stephanie and the Van Sheltons on this ranch. Believe me, not a day goes by that I take my life for granted.

"Our quarter horse business—Stephanie's and mine—has worked out real good. We're a team. I buy, breed, and train the horses, and

Stephanie takes care of the bookkeeping and the business ends. Means a lot to me not to be living off the Van Sheltons' money.

"Now, let's see if you've gotten any better with a rifle."

Chapter Twenty

Two-Tone Skin and Big Knuckles

Greetings from the West, Rebecca:

My dear friend, when I arrived in Wyandotte, I never expected to be spending more time alone with Bram and Jesse than with Frederick. But because Frederick and Doc are the only two physicians in the territory, they're constantly busy. So, I figured I'd better do something about it. And that something turned out to be following along with Frederick on his calls to patients, riding far distances with him in his buggy and putting in long days.

At first I thought he'd be unwilling, worrying whether I could stand what I would witness and also concerned that people might disapprove of us being out unchaperoned. I told him I wasn't worried about either one, and he was glad because he wants me to know what his professional life and his patients are like.

So, for the past five days, I have accompanied him on calls to a variety of patients' homes, ranging from the most humble to those more prosperous. It has been an education, believe me. Also believe me when I say that you and I, as well as all others of our acquaintance, truly live privileged lives, sheltered from the foulness and hardships typical for most of the people I've met this week.

I now understand why Frederick had such a hard time returning to his sanitized medical practice after visiting here several years ago. His knowledge and skills are needed here. Badly.

Rebecca, you have no concept of how very, very hard most of these good people work. The men who farm or ranch from dawn until dusk literally have two-toned skin. The parts exposed to the sun day after day and year after year are the color of mahogany and look as tough as shoe leather. Their unexposed legs, chests and backs—which I've seen helping Frederick examine them—are so white the contrast makes them look sickly.

The women work equally hard and even longer hours, for they must clean up after supper, put the children to bed, and prepare the kitchen for the next day's meals. They clean the house, dig and tend their vegetable garden, churn their butter, sew much of their clothing, prepare the meals, take care of the children, scrub on a washboard, milk the cows, and so many other things. Their hands are rough and scarred, and their knuckles look as big as a man's.

Honestly, they are so worn out from child-bearing and hard labor, many of them die in their forties looking much, much older. They are so isolated that loneliness also takes its toll on them. Even though I'm so different from them, they are openly eager to talk with another woman. I feel so sorry for them, and yet I feel guilty about that because these are proud people who neither want nor appreciate sympathy. They are living the only lives they have ever known.

The Van Sheltons and their friends dwell in an-other world of their own making, much more like ours than many of their less fortunate neighbors. They have gone to great lengths to make my stay a pleasant one, and I have come to love and appreciate all of them.

Fact is, they've gone a little overboard with the gatherings they have organized for me with their friends. Lovely people, all of them, but I'm weary of talking so much about myself. But that's what they want to hear.

Truth be told, I'm homesick for Boston, my fam-ily, my friends, and the great variety of activities. Shop-ping, too. I long to once again purchase something I do not need. I've always done such things guiltlessly, but now I don't know whether I'll be so free in having an-other gown made when my closets are already full of them.

As for marriage with Frederick, I still haven't de-cided. I'm certain I'll never have another proposal from anyone who could measure up to him, but it's bedrock solidly certain he's here to stay. I am running out of time, and he is pressing me for an answer. I am cramming in every experience I can think of to make sure I have a re-alistic knowledge of this town and this part of the coun-try. Confidentially, I have one experience I'm planning just before I leave that will blow you over. If I can pull it off, I'll tell you about it when I get home.

Pray for me because after next month's grand ball at the Van Sheltons' mansion, I'll be returning to Boston. And I cannot leave without facing Frederick with a decision that, one way or the other, will change the entire course of the rest of my life and his.

Sincerely, Honoria

Chapter Twenty-One

The Contessa Rules

Honoria doesn't know whether she is more annoyed or angry. Frederick, clad in his white lab coat, is rocking side to side in his office chair, laughing so hard he can be heard through the closed door to the waiting room.

"You want what?!" he finally is able to reply.

"You heard me, Frederick, and I mean what I said. I want to meet Contessa Bianca, dammit!"

"Wow, you must be serious, Honoria. I've never before heard you use even a mild form of cursing. All right, I'll take you seriously. But you know I have to ask why in the world you would want to meet a woman who operates a house of prostitution?"

"Well, it's not because I am seeking employment, Frederick," Honoria retorts, her words and expression loaded with sarcasm. "I have my reasons, curiosity not being the least of them. And that's all you need to know. Now, are you going to arrange a meeting for me, or do I ask Bram? He'll do it, you know."

"Oh, yeah, I have no doubt about that. OK, I'll see if the Contessa is willing. Don't suppose you also want to meet her at the Gentleman's Club?"

"I'd like that, Frederick, if I had the power to make myself invisible. I'd love to see the inside of that place—how it looks, how the girls act around their clients and that sort of thing. But, no, I know we'll have to meet in a more discreet location. So, when can you do this?"

"I'll ask her tomorrow," Frederick promises. "Everyone knows Doc and I go there regularly for medical reasons, so that gives me a good enough excuse. I'll be in touch. "

As Honoria rises from her chair to leave, smiling now that she has gotten her way, she hears Frederick whisper, more to himself than to her: "Just when you think you know somebody . . . ."

***

Three days later, Honoria discovers Frederick is right in his description of the Contessa, She is undeniably extraordinary. Her figure is indeed marvelous, her outfit is expensive and in the best of fashion and style. It is form-fitting, black and white striped, yet conservative. Her hat is wide-brimmed, white with a narrow black band and a complementary red bow.

Honoria feels underdressed. She is wearing a riding outfit, having traveled to town on Crown Prince, accompanied by Bram, who is having his horse shod while Honoria completes her "shopping." He doesn't suspect the pretext she is using for going to town. Not that he would disapprove; indeed, he would be perversely amused.

The two women, so thoroughly different they might as well be from separate planets, eye each other for a few moments as only females can. Curiosity reaches its peak.

"Frederick is right about you, Contessa," Honoria observes.

"You mean because I am an albino?" the Contessa infers.

"Partly," Honoria confesses. "But only partly. I've rarely seen a woman with a more thoroughly feminine figure or one clothed more beautifully than you. I am glad you agreed to meet me. Thank you for coming to Frederick's office, especially at this early hour."

"You're welcome, Honoria. Besides, I must say I am as curious about meeting you as you are me. I'm eager to know about you and your doctor. But other than getting a good look, what else do you expect of me?'

"More than you might guess," Honoria replies. "But let's get to know each other a little better, then I'll tell you why, if that's agreeable with you."

"Fine with me, Honoria. You start first. Tell me about your background, how you met your Frederick, and what your plans are. Then I'll tell you about me, or at least as much as you want to hear. After all, I am a prostitute, you know."

"I'm afraid I'm not very interesting, Contessa. Except for extensive travel in the East and abroad, I've lived my entire life in New England. My family is wealthy, and I am terribly spoiled and pampered. I'm educated, but I've never had to work. I have no job, only the expectation of my family that I will marry someone of my social class, have two or three children and carry on our way of life. I'm afraid I am quite boring."

"Not to me, Honoria. Your way of life sounds like a beautiful dream to me. Tell me a little more about your family, and then get to Dr. Carlisle. Frankly, if you don't mind my saying so, he is dazzling. So handsome, intelligent, well spoken, charming. And kind, especially kind and non-judgmental."

"He is all that, I acknowledge. Every woman—as well as most men—would agree with you, Contessa. To answer your first question, my parents are wonderful, and I have one older brother, who is president of my family's shipping line, and one older married sister with two children we all adore. I'm not so spoiled that I don't realize and appreciate that I am blessed.

"I am twenty-three years old, an old-maid by many families' standards. I've had a number of proposals from men of prominent

151

backgrounds, but they lack the character Frederick has. Frederick can be fun, but he is a serious physician. Even though he is terribly wealthy and from one of the finest families in New England, he wants to be of service, especially to those who otherwise might suffer because they could never afford or have access to a doctor with his education and skills. His genuine goodness is what I love most about him."

"But how did you meet? How did you become his fiancé?" the Contessa asks, leading Honoria to the part of her life the Contessa is most curious about.

"Basically, I suppose, because our families have been friends for generations, and, consequently, we are part of the same social groups. And, as you agree, Frederick is gorgeous, charming and all the rest. Every girl wanted him. Why he chose me, I have only one clue.

"As you may know, Frederick and Stephanie Van Shelton seemed destined for each other until things happened with Jesse Bodine, the man she gave up Frederick for. Frederick then 'settled' for me. But that part I will save until I hear about you, Contessa."

"Not much to tell, Honoria. Our lives are direct opposites. I was born poor. My mother was an albino 'freak' in a carnival sideshow, and I never knew my father. My sister and I were also seen as freaks and were the objects of much staring, pointing, and derision. Our only friends were from the carnival, and after our mother died when we were teen-agers, we left the show to find better-paying work. But the only kind that paid enough to keep us and allow us to buy books to educate our-selves was prostitution. Men were oddly attracted to us.

"I never wanted to marry or have children because I didn't want an-other child to suffer my fate. My sister wasn't bitter as I was. Somehow she was—and is—a sweet girl. In fact, she is married and expecting a baby, that, incidentally, Dr. Carlisle tells me should be born normal be-cause her husband is normal.

"Despite all these handicaps, I discovered I am smart. I educated—and continue to educate—myself through books, and a few fortunate associations with intelligent men—clients, really—who have mentored me. I eventually saved enough money to open my business, and I have become wealthy.

"That's about it, Honoria. The unvarnished truth. Now, tell me why else you wanted to meet me. I assure you I am sincerely interested."

"Honestly, Contessa, I am going to spend a lot of time thinking about what you already have told me. I won't insult you by saying I feel sorry for you. Quite the contrary; I admire you.

"What I want to know may not shock you, but it would astound everyone else who knows me, including—and perhaps especially—Frederick. Contessa, I am a twenty-three-year-old virgin. I know nothing about sexual relations with a man, other than what I have read or what little my young married friends have been willing to share. Which is very little because most knew no more than I did before they married.

"You see, Frederick did 'settle' for me. He loved Stephanie passionately, but he and I both realize that although we love each other, it hasn't reached the level of passion, at least not for him. We otherwise are a near-perfect match.

"What I want from you—if you are willing—is tutoring, for lack of a better word. What I know virtually nothing about, I suspect you know all about. And that is," Honoria says, blushing from embarrassment but determined to ask, "what to do to please a man sexually and what not to do. I really know nothing except how to submit and let a man do the rest."

"Hmm. You've caught me off guard, Honoria. This I did not anticipate. But, believe it or not, you are not the first lady to make such an inquiry.

"This may not be in the proper order, but here goes, nevertheless. Let's call these 'The Contessa Rules,' based upon my experience in the business and what I have learned about pleasing clients.

"First, it's perfectly all right for proper women like you to enjoy sex. It's not something to be endured as a wifely duty. Females are taught that nonsense as children in hopes of keeping them from engaging in sex before marriage, although the goal is understandable. Men enjoy it; why shouldn't we?

"Second, because husbands and wives aren't always in the mood at the same time, sex is not always mutually enjoyable. Do it anyway. You'll both be happier and more content in the long run.

"Third, along those same lines, don't avoid sex with obviously untruthful excuses like the proverbial headache. If you just can't bear it at the time, say so, but make sure your husband knows it's no reflection on him or his abilities. He'll be disappointed, but he'll respect your honesty.

"Fourth, even ladies should occasionally initiate sex, not always leave the first move up to the husband. Men like that. Makes them feel desirable and masculine. Remember, it doesn't take much to get men in the mood: a sexy look, a come-hither smile, an intimate touch. Even if such things do not always lead to sex, I think they are essential in a good marriage. Daily hugs and kisses and saying 'I love you' cost nothing, but they pay incalculable dividends.

"Finally, wives could put me and people like me out of the 'husband business' if they learned to be active sexual partners instead of lifeless receivers who pray that sex will be as infrequent and as short-lasting as possible."

"Whew!" Honoria exclaims. I'm both emboldened and frightened by what you've taught me, Contessa."

"You'll be fine, believe me, Honoria. And even though there is a great deal more to marriage than sex, a marriage without it is just an arrangement. You and Dr. Gorgeous deserve better.

"And now I have to go before the staff and the patients start arriving. It has been a real pleasure, Honoria."

"Likewise, Contessa. But I'm afraid I got the best of the bargain; I also received an invaluable education—one I have no doubt will be the most candid and honest lesson I'll ever learn."

Chapter Twenty-Two

For the Second Time

For the second time in four years, Frederick and his partner have the honor of leading off the dancing at one of Mrs. Van Shelton's grand balls. Only this time, it is Honoria, not Stephanie, he is guiding gracefully around the hardwood maple floor. As he smiles and nods at the admiring onlookers, Frederick can't help remembering it was on a fateful night similar to this he lost Stephanie to Jesse Bodine. However, his future with the woman he loves is not threatened this night by another man. His rival is geography.

"Enjoying yourself?" Frederick asks. "This is all for you, you know."

"Oh, yes. Yes, I am. I feel a little conspicuous, but I'm reveling in it all. My gown is the most beautiful one in the room, and I'm dancing with the handsomest man in Wyandotte. A woman doesn't get many chances like this to be on display. So let them get an eyeful if they want!"

As always, Mrs. Van Shelton has created so much splendor it is overwhelming. With the capable help of Stephanie, Lillian, and a large staff of full-time and part-time employees, she has provided a tastefully decorated room featuring seasonal flowers placed strategically around the huge hall with streamers hanging from the ceiling in complex, intertwined patterns. The walls have been repainted in pastel yellows and greens to complement Honoria's elegant Cinderella-style gown. The guests are in a jovial mood following a champagne reception and a full-course dinner as scrumptious and as impressive as it was meant to be by the San Francisco chef Mrs. Van Shelton paid a small fortune to prepare.

Attending are family friends and local dignitaries, most of whom Honoria has met during her three-month stay. The only face in the crowd she is surprised to see is that of a man who detests such events. It is Bram, and he not only is attending, but he also is wearing formal attire he swore he would never be caught dead in.

"If I should die while wearing these clothes, promise you won't bury me in them," he jokes to his father.

"You look good, son. You are my son, are you not? I'm still not convinced it's really you all spiffied up," his father laughs.

Honoria is delighted to see Bram, for she is very fond of this family rebel who accompanied her on the last fifty miles of her trip West, bought her Crown Prince, chaperoned her trips to town, and made himself available anytime she wanted to ride her handsome horse around the ranch. She smiles with considerable satisfaction to witness Bram's one obvious holdout against tradition: He is wearing a bolo tie with a large turquoise setting in heavy silver with matching metal at the end of each of the two cords.

As for Bram, his authentically tough, often crude manner more suited for a barroom than a ballroom is conspicuously absent tonight. His heart is in his throat as he observes this "hell of a woman" who is the center of attention. He won't admit he is as close to being in love as he has ever come because it can't work. And he knows it. Still, he is determined to live this night for what it is worth and dance with her at his first opportunity.

"Honoria looks lovely, doesn't she?" Stephanie says as she hands her brother a cup of punch she knows he won't drink. It is her excuse to see his reaction to her question. Bram hasn't hidden his feelings for Honoria very effectively from the rest of the family.

"Looks right nice," Bram concedes, saying nothing more.

"Going to dance with her, Bram?" Stephanie needles.

"Just as soon as I can pry her away from 'Dr. Gorgeous.'" Bram has learned from his frequent visits to The Gentlemen's Club the Countess's pet name for Frederick. Stephanie smiles quizzically but asks nothing more.

Frederick, too, is determined Honoria will dance the night away, having an experience she will always remember. Earlier in the week, he persuaded Doc to sacrifice his attendance by staying in town in case of an emergency. Frederick has disappointed Honoria enough by his absences caused by his medical practice. "Nothing short of an epidemic will call me away from this ball," he promised her.

And he is true to his word. He and Honoria meet every request, dancing with husbands and wives of friends, the Bodines, the Van Sheltons—Bram included—and to their great delight, Esther and Jonathan.

The evening goes perfectly. Even the nagging pressure of Honoria's decision has temporarily receded.

Chapter Twenty-Three

Time for "The Talk"

"So, Lillian, are you ready for us to have 'The Talk,'" Honoria asks almost casually over afternoon tea on the Van Sheltons' flower-lined veranda.

"Oh, goodness, my friend. I've been expecting it for some time, but I must admit I'm probably more anxious about it than you. You've kept your thoughts to yourself during the months you have been in Wyandotte, and I know you are leaving us soon."

"Yes, I'll depart for Boston within the next few days. And although I'm sorry to put the responsibility of 'The Talk' on you, I'm sure you have known all along you're the only one who has the experience to advise me. You will help me, won't you?" Honoria pleads more than asks.

"Of course, Honoria. But let me make clear from the outset that I sincerely hope you will marry Freddy and move here. Let me also make clear that I have an ulterior motive: Having you close by as a dear friend, especially considering the similarities of our backgrounds, would make my life much richer.

"So, let's hear it. You talk first. All you want. Then I'll reply as honestly, as candidly, and as objectively as I am capable of doing,"

Honoria draws a deep breath, pats Lillian's hand twice for courage, and lifts the gate that has been damming her thoughts from the time Frederick invited her to Wyandotte.

"Do I love Frederick? Yes, almost desperately.

"Do I want to marry him and have his children? Yes, without any doubts about that part.

"Do I like him? Yes, as much as I love him. And, Lillian, liking him is absolutely essential for me. I'm wise enough to know that's far more important, far more lasting than the haze of the passionate honeymoon period.

"Do I respect him simply as a person? Totally. He's is a wonderful man with perhaps the most admirable of professions. Because of his wealth, he could do only those things he finds pleasing and pleasurable; yet he has studied long and diligently to acquire the knowledge he needs to relieve the pain and suffering of his fellow human beings.

"Do I like his friends, and do I think I could be part of that circle? I love his friends. You, Ruben, precious Esther and Jonathan, Stephanie and Jesse, Mr. and Mrs. Van Shelton, and, of course, Doc. And, perhaps shockingly, I adore Bram. I was warned by most of you he would be so difficult and unrefined. But, Lillian, no one has treated me better than Bram. I think he's wonderful. Yes, I think I could fit quite comfortably into that circle.

"Now, the big question, the one with which I am struggling with my entire heart, mind, and soul. Frederick has transformed his life. But can I? Can I give up a life I love in Boston? My parents and my siblings? My lifelong friends? The lovely luncheons, dinner parties, the theater, the opera, the shopping for fine clothes, the travel, and being the focus of attention so much of the time?

"Honestly, I don't know. What would I do with my time in Wyandotte, Lillian? In addition to your husband, you have your children and the Bodines and Mr. and Mrs. Van Shelton. I would not have that. I would not even have your company all that often, given the twenty-mile round trip from town.

"Frederick will be working most days. He is subject to going out on calls at night, even staying overnight at patients' homes while he attends to them. I would be totally alone much of the time.

"How could I stand it?" Honoria asks, pushing back her chair and lifting her palms upward in a gesture of frustrated perplexity.

Lillian rises to her feet, places her hands on her cheeks, and rocks back and forth for a few moments, praying for guidance, for she knows her words may have a profound effect not only on the lives of Honoria and Frederick but also many others, both here and in Boston.

"Honoria, I realize you expect me to know the answers, and perhaps the solutions, you are so desperately seeking. I hardly know where to begin or in what order to express my thoughts. So, let me start by telling you of my experience with Ruben.

"I fell deeply in love with Ruben when he was attending law school in Cambridge. I was convinced he was almost perfect for me—with one enormous exception. He was unshakable in his determination to return to Nevada for good. So, even though I had never been west of the Mississippi River, let alone to what seemed to me to be some God-forsaken wilderness, I gave in and married him in my dream wedding in Boston. We had a fairy-tale honeymoon in Europe, and I was as happy as I could possibly be.

"Then came the west. Oh, my God, it was so desolate, so isolated— worse than I could ever have imagined. Even living in that magnificent mansion didn't help. I cried myself to sleep every night the first month here. I'm sure Ruben wished he had abandoned me in London or in Paris. I was the worst wife imaginable. I made the entire household miserable."

"But you stayed, Lillian. What made you stay?"

"My love for Ruben, and," Lillian admitted with embarrassment, "my forcing him to agree that I could spend every summer back in New England with my parents, my siblings, and my friends—a promise he has faithfully kept, even after Jonathan and Esther were born.

"Gradually I fit in. My in-laws are so wonderful, Ruben is very successful in handling his family's business affairs with his father, and the children are happy. I have made some dear friends in the community, and Marissa loves nothing better than organizing parties and dances for us. I teach the children at home, and when Ruben's business trips take him to cities like San Francisco, I frequently accompany him.

"All in all, I have a good life here. But there is no doubt, Honoria, that it's nothing like my previous life in the East. I'm not saying one is necessarily better than the other, but the difference is enormous.

"I can't promise you that you'll adjust and be as happy as I am. Only you can figure that out."

"But, Lillian, I don't know. I don't know, and I'm scared to death of making a choice I'll regret the rest of my life. But, you're right about the decision. No one can make it for me."

The two women stand, wrap their arms around each other and say nothing more.

There is nothing more to be said.

Chapter Twenty-Four

A Bold Move and "The Decision"

There is one additional experience Honoria considers essential before returning to her life in Boston. She has been planning it continually for weeks. It is a decision she has reached entirely on her own, for there is no one in Wyandotte—not even the Contessa—or in Boston, or anywhere in between with whom she can share it or seek counsel. She is certain of only one thing: No one who loves her would approve—perhaps not even Frederick.

Because the stage is leaving early, Honoria persuades Frederick to let her spend her last night at his house and office, overcoming his objections to the damage her reputation might suffer if the good people of Wyandotte ever heard about such an unseemly arrangement.

"You live in a building divided into two distinct parts, Frederick. Everybody knows that. I'll sleep on the office couch, my honor safely segregated away downstairs from your living quarters on the second floor."

It's an argument Frederick knows no man can win. He reluctantly agrees. They have as close to an intimate dinner as is possible at the hotel restaurant and afterward walk hand-in-hand to his house. Frederick wants to settle matters, but Honoria puts him off.

"This evening has been so pleasant, Frederick. We can get up early, have a leisurely breakfast at the hotel, and talk all you want." She kisses him lightly on the lips, pushes him firmly toward his quarters and says good night.

Frederick, like most good men, gives in once again, swallowing his disappointment about being put off on the talk and being granted one solitary kiss that is no more than a brush of their lips. And, like most men good and bad, he fails to see what's coming.

***

Trembling with apprehension and excitement, Honoria leaves her bed directly after midnight, walks soundlessly up the stairs to Frederick's bedroom door, slowly and quietly opens it halfway, and turns her eyes toward the sleeping body of her fiancé. The room is partly illuminated by the moonlight penetrating the space between the draperies, providing sufficient light for her to edge toward the bed. She gazes lovingly at Frederick, pausing to appreciate his handsome, masculine form, clad only in pajama bottoms.

She extends her left arm to his right shoulder and presses it gently until he awakens. She waits as his eyes adjust to the faint light, then touches her right index finger vertically to his lips, for she wants no words to pass between them. He turns on his side to gain full sight of her, providing the precise moment she has anticipated. She looks directly into his beautiful pale blue eyes. and confidently, without the slightest embarrassment or awkwardness, pulls the ties at the top of each shoulder, and frees her nightgown to glide gracefully to the floor, revealing a generous but taut body so thoroughly feminine that it would arouse any man still breathing.

Frederick lifts the sheet invitingly, and they pull into each other's arms.

***

A little before daylight, Honoria slips quietly out of Frederick's bed, taking care not to awaken him. She wants to freshen herself and be appropriately clothed for her departure. She has her bags packed and is sitting patiently in the outer room when she hears Frederick say, "Good morning."

Neither mentions what transpired between them during the night. For the time being, it speaks for itself.

"Good morning to you," Honoria says a little too cheerfully, hoping to mask her anxiety over the answer she must soon give to Fredrick. "What are the chances of your taking a lady to breakfast at the hotel?"

"About one hundred percent, I'd say," Frederick replies. "Your treat or mine?" he kids, his optimism evident in his voice.

Frederick is dressed in less than a half hour, and both feel rejuvenated by the brisk early morning air during the brief walk to the restaurant. Neither is particularly hungry, and they finally get around to the question they knew from the beginning of her visit they eventually would have to face. For his part, Frederick has been heroically patient. But now the time had come. Honoria will be departing within the hour.

"Frederick it pains me, literally, to say this, but the truth is, I do not think I can live here without eventually making both of our lives wretched. I do love you, and your friends. Everyone has been so marvelous and honest with me. But I'm convinced I'll make you unhappy."

Considering what transpired between them just hours ago, Frederick cannot believe her words. "You did talk with Lillian, didn't you, Honoria?" Frederick asks, his concern and disappointment so hurtfully obvious. "I thought you were giving me your answer in my bedroom last night. Tell me what the barriers are. I'm willing to meet almost any request you could make of me, including your spending three months a year in New England, the same as Lillian and her children."

"Frederick, I cannot envision the kind of life I would have in Wyandotte. Other than being your wife—which I know should be enough in itself—I would be virtually isolated. Our best friends live too far just to drop in on.

"Your work keeps you very busy and your hours are so unpredictable. You missed many of the get-togethers we should have had during my three months here. It's not your fault; it's the demands of your profession. But I need a husband I can count on to be present for anniversaries, children's birthdays, recitals, and graduations. I do not want to be both mother and father to my children while my husband is absent, no matter how noble the reasons.

"Other than church, there are no social activities in town for me. In Boston, I have a full life. Here, when I'm not with you or getting an occasional visit from one or more of our friends, I would have nothing to do. Outside of marriage, my life would be pointless. Even after we had children, as much as I would love and care for them, I wouldn't want you and them to be my entire life. Not to mention the educational and social opportunities they would have in a big city. And I cannot even tolerate the thought of sending them off to boarding school. I want my children to grow up in a house with both a father and a mother regularly present.

"I know it's useless to ask you to reconsider going back with me. You have chosen the life you want. I must do the same. God forgive me if I'm being self-centered and selfish. But you deserve the truth, Frederick. And there it is."

"Then chances are not good that you will reconsider and marry me, even if I give you more time?" Frederick whispers, as if he were taking his last breath. "Then please, Honoria, help me understand what last night was all about."

"It was about neither of us going to our graves without fully expressing our love for each other. That I would deeply, bitterly regret for the rest of my life, and I think you would, too. Now we'll never need to."

Those words are her last to Frederick. Feeling deeply conflicted and desperately overwhelmed by what has just passed between them, Honoria takes Frederick's right hand in both of hers, kisses his palm tenderly, walks alone out the door, and, as far as they know, out of the other's life forever.

The next face Honoria sees is Bram's as he helps her into the stage-coach and joins her for the fifty-mile trip to the railway station. Bram takes notice of the tears Honoria is unable to restrain and wisely offers only small talk until he sees her safely onto the train for her sad trip back home.

Within two months, Honoria is married, accepting—or rather settling for—the Boston blueblood whose proposal she had declined a few months earlier. Seven months later, she gives birth to a healthy son.

Part 3

Fifteen Years Later

The Transformation of Wyandotte

"It burns me up that I can buy and sell every one of those pissant broom-pushers and saloon-swabbers, but even the lowliest of them take walking for granted and can produce snotty-nosed kids with no more effort than it takes to drop their drawers."

Chapter One

The Reigning Stallion

As regular as clockwork, several dozen habitual gawkers exit the shops, restaurants, and supply stores of downtown Wyandotte for their weekday ritual, just as they have for the past four years. They are joined by curious visitors who follow Pied Piper-like from the hotel, not knowing quite what to expect, but determined not to be left out of whatever is about to transpire.

They do not have to wait long. At precisely nine a.m., they observe the arrival on Main Street of the most ostentatious open carriage they have ever seen. It is deep black with several coatings of lacquer that reflect the early morning sun. A multi-colored family crest of dubious authenticity adorns each side door, and overstuffed red leather seats boost the passengers to throne height. A pair of sleek black horses in plumed headdress and heavy silver harness are driven by a tall, broad-shouldered coachman in formal coat, top hat, and knee-high boots.

Its occupants are a man and a woman. Their dress is painstakingly elaborate, purposely designed to be conspicuous. Their attire is accentuated by a showy assemblage of oversized diamond rings, stickpins, and bracelets sparkling from every appendage the human body can respectably expose. Altogether, it makes for a quite a show, one meticulously calculated to impress, provoke envy, and leave no doubt that the couple are pearls among swine.

The man is a power in Wyandotte. His wealth and the underhanded methods he uses to acquire his money make him the most hated and the most feared of the town's movers and shakers. His young woman is the most extraordinarily beautiful and desirable his considerable fortune can buy, and he misses no opportunity to flaunt her face and body before every other man, leaving no doubt that he has positioned himself as the reigning stallion of the herd, and the others presumably must make do with his leavings.

The show ends when the driver stops, not in front of the finest office building in Wyandotte but behind it, shielded from view in the alley.

Thirty-one-year-old Preston Turner, you see, acknowledges to no one that he cannot descend his own carriage without help.

***

Although Doc and Frederick do not leave their breakfast to join the onlookers on the sidewalk, they can see from The Silver Queen Hotel's front windows the perverse satisfaction Preston gets every time he puts himself and Jolene on display. The two physicians have seen it all before. Many times. And they react, as usual, with both revulsion and guilt. They've never fully forgiven themselves for the kind of man Preston Turner has turned out to be.

"You've heard all this before, Frederick," Doc says, laying down his fork, his appetite stunted. "He was one of the nicest kids in this part of the country: polite, respectful, hard-working, thoroughly dependable. Then the damned accident with that bronco and his father's needless death the boy caused himself, at least indirectly.

"Now he's eaten up with guilt and bitterness and is taking out his revenge against everybody and everything. Seems to me he's determined to spend his every waking moment proving that even if he is incapable of walking, running, mounting a horse or a woman, he's more man than any of us."

"Damn shame, Doc," Frederick replies. "I earnestly thought we'd headed him in the right direction fifteen years ago when you and I, along with Mr. Van Shelton, Ruben, Bram, Jesse, and his old foreman Duggin, got him to start moving again after his father's funeral.

"I mean, after all, he did follow our advice. He spent two years being tutored by Harvey Barrett in all aspects of the bookkeeping end of running a big cattle ranch. Mr. Van Shelton and Ruben taught him how to do the buying and selling, and he learned from Bram, Jesse, and Duggin everything he needs to know about the everyday operations on the range. I'm convinced when Preston took over after he turned eighteen, he was well prepared."

"All that's undeniably true, Frederick," Doc allows. "But, medically, he's regressed, especially mentally, as you know from watching him yourself. Oh, back then when we were helping him, he was polite and attentive enough. But he never laughed. Never took any joy out of anything—except seeing his father's sizable fortune grow. We didn't recognize the signs then, Frederick, but it's become clear to all of us Preston was gathering his power for plans only he knew about. Now look at him."

"Yeah, I don't need reminding, Doc. He controls most of the big spreads, which he got by lending money to ranchers and farmers at usurious rates when they couldn't qualify for conventional loans and then foreclosing on them when they couldn't pay him back. Then there's the two saloons, the general store, the livery stable, and, if rumors are true, he's also the silent owner of two whorehouses and is trying to put the Contessa out of business."

"Bizarre as hell how life works, isn't it Frederick? On one ordinary morning a boy from a wonderful, happy, prosperous family gets stomped by a horse and the hellish consequences keep falling like dominoes all these years later. I'll be a son-of-a-bitch if I can understand it!"

"Maybe it's best not even to try, Doc. Life does whatever it does, and we just deal with it. Sometimes we're given no choice."

***

While he was enjoying lording it over the townsfolk, Preston spotted the two doctors through the hotel window. They stay on his mind as his coachman and two other male assistants get him situated in his office seat, a structure disguised by a master craftsman not to look like the wheelchair its owner needs to get around.

"I hate those two bastards," he spews venomously at Jolene, who is accustomed to serving as his sounding board, among her other duties.

"Who, Preston? What two men are you talking about?" she responds in a tone she has trained to sound interested and respectful without being judgmental.

"Doc and Frederick, that's who!" he shouts. "And you know why, Jolene. All the time I was growing up, Doc pretended to be my friend. And when Dr. Carlisle came along, he acted like he really cared about me. Well, if they cared so much, why am I still half a man? Doc's been practicing medicine for decades, and Frederick graduated from one of the best schools in the country. Big damn deal! They didn't know enough between them to help me. Even worse, they led me on with false hope.

"Every time we ride through this pathetic town, I'm reminded how much I've been robbed of. It burns me up that I can buy and sell every one of those pissant broom-pushers and saloon-swabbers watching us, but even the lowliest of them take walking for granted and can produce snotty-nosed kids with no more effort than it takes to drop their drawers.

"Well, to hell with them. You hear me? To hell with all of them!"

Jolene is long accustomed to the ravings and rantings of this man who, in effect, bought her when she was eighteen years old, making her the equivalent of an indentured servant with no real work to perform. She fit almost perfectly Preston's shopping list of criteria his "recruiters" were ordered to follow:

> She must be a New Englander to match the background of Lillian and Honoria.
> She must be young.
> She must be not just beautiful but drop-dead gorgeous.
> She must be "purchasable"; that is, her family must be so desperate she will be willing to sacrifice herself for their sake.

Jolene came close enough to be recommended. Her family is a couple of notches below Lillian's and Honoria's in social standing and fortune but not enough to make a difference in Wyandotte, Nevada. Her middle-aged father had recently succumbed smack in the middle of a financial crisis in his business, and his stunned, heartbroken family was about to lose everything. Her mother has no income of her own, and Jolene's two siblings are still children.

Preston's agents, including a lawyer from a leading Boston firm, struck the deal. The contract includes many details Preston insisted on, but it primarily provides generously for Jolene's mother, sister, and brother. They get to keep their very fine home and have a monthly allowance more than enough to exceed all their needs, including schooling at a prestigious private academy. In return, Jolene will live with Preston, and unless he stipulates otherwise, she must be constantly at his side day and night, and do whatever he requires.

The contract further states she is not to see her family or have any other communication with them; she may not have visitors or leave his residence or office without his permission and one of his men as a chaperone; she is to have no romantic or sexual involvement with any other man; she is to look her best at all times; and she is to be publicly affectionate to Preston whenever he wants to make others envious.

In return, she will be treated with as much respect and kindness as he has to give under the circumstances, and, most importantly for Jolene, the contract will expire after five years with a fifty thousand dollar settlement for her and her family.

After a long, tearful discussion with her mother, Jolene accepted. Her convincing argument was the five-year limitation. She will be only twenty-three and still have a full life ahead of her—if she can keep her past from catching up with her.

Chapter Two

Wyandotte Courts the Great Western Railroad

Eight men and one woman sit at the long conference table in the room adjacent to the Van Sheltons' office at the Golden Eagle Ranch. Each has the wealth and the influence to have a say in Wyandotte's future. Collectively, they have the potential to transform the growing town into a booming city. It is no exaggeration to claim they have gathered this day to change the course of history for western Nevada. Their means to that end is the Great Western Railroad.

Wyandotte is positioned to compete with two other similar towns for the grand prize of a railhead that would enable their community to spread its means of transportation and commerce in a variety of directions. Wyandotte would prosper greatly, as would those with big money to invest.

"Thank you all for being here. I very much appreciate your willingness to meet as a group," Mr. Van Shelton says in his welcome. "We all know one another, so there's no need for introductions. We also all know why we are here, and your very presence indicates we can start by agreeing we all want that railhead, if we can meet Great Western's terms. Obviously, because there are competitors other than us, the railroad owners are sitting in the catbird's seat. No question about that; they hold most of the bargaining chips.

"Now, Ruben has been analyzing Great Western's demands, so I'll step aside and let him lay them out for us. Ruben . . . ."

"Thank you, father. Friends, after much study and thought, I realistically believe we can beat our competitors and win that railhead if we can pool enough of our resources to guarantee we can deliver the following:

"1. The land needed for a right of way that will enable the fifty-mile rail line to be built as swiftly and as inexpensively as possible.

"2. Top-quality housing for the railroad executives who would be stationed here.

"3. The addition of probably two hotels to the one we now have.

"4. A large fenced area next to the rail line where we can hold cattle prior to shipment. That means, of course, we can expect Wyandotte to be a terminal for cattle drives from near and far.

"5. The building of a hospital large enough to have separate wards for men, women, and children, plus half a dozen private rooms for wealthier citizens who will demand such treatment.

"6. A fully staffed bank with a safe comparable to those used in big-city institutions.

"7. A law enforcement system with sufficiently trained personnel to handle the influx of settlers, visitors, and the—shall we say 'energetic'—cowhands who will want to celebrate the end of their cattle drives.

"8. A school system expanded from the eighth grade through high school.

"Those are the certain demands. There may be others."

"Say, Ruben, what's your estimate of the initial investment for all that," Gertrude Jamison, a big ranch owner and the only female in the group, asks.

"Conservatively, about three-quarters of a million dollars, Gertrude. It could be more."

"Are you suggesting our group of nine come up with all the money," Roy Stephenson, a partner in a silver mine operation, inquires.

"No, Roy," Ruben replies. "Obviously, the more each of us invests, the bigger return we can expect on our money. But I do not think it would be wise for us to fund it all, even if we wanted to. We need to leave room for smaller investors to ensure widespread community support, as well as to give our citizens of more modest means a chance to improve themselves and their families financially. A larger base of investors will also appeal to the railroad, I think. They'd see the strength of the community behind us, and that alone could give us the edge over our competitors."

"Just how do you envision our investments working, Ruben?" Perry Meadows, owner of a big cattle spread, asks.

"We have several choices, Perry. We can form a corporation and own everything jointly—railroad stock, hotels, restaurants, and so forth. Or we each could own one or more of those entities separately. Whichever we choose, I think we have to make certain no one like Preston Turner, for example, can buy them up one by one from us and gain majority control of the holdings and thereby, in effect, 'own' the city.

"We can figure out these details in subsequent meetings. And that brings me to our biggest and most forceful obstacle to making any of this work. And that's the man whose name I just mentioned. Preston Turner got word of our meeting and sent his lawyer, Randolph Grafton, to talk with me yesterday afternoon. It's no understatement to say he delivered not only a list of demands but also a genuine threat from Preston."

"Just where the hell does that crazy little shit get off making demands, and what is it he wants?" Bram insists on knowing, his anger making clear he takes Preston's threats personally.

"First, Bram, let's not underestimate Preston. As we all know, he's very wealthy and he is ruthless in getting what he wants. We have plenty of proof of that. Unfortunately, he's holding some strong options, and he wants in on everything."

"Just what, other than his fortune, does Turner have to use against us, Ruben?" another of the potential investors wants to know.

"His lawyer showed me proof that Preston holds deeds to more than half of the fifty miles of land the railroad needs for the lines. He may have a warped mind, but he's smart and he's forward looking. He anticipated the day would come when the railroad would expand in our area, and he figured out the general directions the track would have to go and bought up the land, piece by piece."

"Well, Ruben, what does he want?" Mr. Van Shelton asks.

"Half a million dollars in cash for the land, which he knows we won't pay, or an equal partnership in our corporation and separate ownership of the holding area for the cattle awaiting shipment. Obviously, if he can get that, he figures he can control the sales between the cattlemen and the railroad."

"Damn!" Mr. Van Shelton spouts. "Friends, it seems clear we can't avoid involving Preston. But we need to think this through thoroughly and come up with a wise plan of action—one that absolutely cuts that scoundrel in for the smallest piece possible while developing an ironclad method of keeping him from devising ways to turn us against one another and force control out of our hands.

"I propose we adjourn and gather back here in five days, and in the interim have Ruben meet with Preston's lawyer and see what's the least we can settle for."

The others agree and file out of the room considerably less enthusiastic and optimistic than when they entered an hour earlier.

Preston Turner has positioned himself solidly. He flexed his muscles this day before the most powerful and influential members of the community, and as he gleefully anticipated, they know full well they must respect his strength.

Chapter Three

A Potential Ally

"You look worried, my dear," Lillian says as Ruben enters the schoolroom a few minutes after she has completed her lessons for the day with the children. "Did the meeting go badly?"

"Yes and no, Lillian. Yes, you are right that I am worried, and no, the meeting went rather well actually, insofar as the people there are concerned."

"How so, Ruben?"

"Well, I think we and our friends are of one mind about competing for the railhead. We all want it. We think it would be good for Wyandotte and its people. We definitely have the money, along with an almost ideal location, and it promises to be an excellent investment."

"Then what's worrying you?"

"Preston Turner, Lillian, Preston Turner. We found out yesterday he has bought the land rights to more than half the route the railway would take, and that gives him, in effect, the upper hand with us, at least for the time being."

"He's blackmailing us, then?"

"I think Preston would call it bargaining with a closed fist instead of a handshake, Lillian. He's demanding a far bigger piece of the pie than we dare risk under his control. Our group is going to meet again in a few days, and it's up to me in the interim to bargain things down with his lawyer."

"With his lawyer, Ruben? Why not with Preston himself?"

"Because that's the way Preston's mind works. He'll not deal with us personally yet because that would mean he would have to look up to me and the others from his wheelchair. That he will not do. At least not until he has humiliated us to the point where he is in total, unchallengeable control."

"What an awful, hateful man, my dear. Why does he dislike us and the others so? What did our family, as well as Doc and Frederick and the others, ever do to harm him?"

"Lillian, Preston's mind is so poisoned by his accident and his father's death he despises the world. I suppose the only person who can stand him is that Jolene woman."

"Not even her, if my guess is right, Ruben."

Surprised by his wife's judgment, Ruben asks, "And just how would you figure that, my love? Do you know something I should know?"

"I don't know about that, but I can tell you what she said to me yesterday when I was shopping in town."

"You actually talked with her?"

"I certainly did, and if you had been a fly on the wall, my dear, here is almost word-for-word what you would have witnessed."

"Good morning, Jolene. I'm Lillian Van Shelton. Hope you don't mind my interrupting your shopping."

Startled to be spoken to in public by a lady of prominence, Jolene blushes but recovers enough of her composure to say, "Not at all, Mrs. Van Shelton. I know who you are. I've admired you and your lovely family on other occasions when I've seen you in town."

"And we have admired you, Jolene. And as I am calling you by your first name, please call me Lillian. By the way, I do not know your last name."

181

"It's Lloyd. My family is from New England, and I can tell from your accent that's something we have in common."

"Yes, my maiden name is Wellesley, and my family is from Boston."

"Oh, I see," Jolene says. "Your family is well known."

"Well, not in the West," Lillian laughs. "Out here, people take me for a native until I open my mouth and sound 'foreign.'"

Lillian notices Jolene's eyes glancing nervously, as if she is being watched. A large man standing conspicuously in the corner of this women's clothing store is making no effort to conceal his attention.

"I suppose you're long accustomed to men staring at you, Jolene. I must say I can't blame them. You are indeed the most beautiful woman I've ever seen. I mean, I'm a woman, and I cannot keep my eyes off you."

"That's all God's doing, Lillian. Not mine, and, believe me, it is more of a curse than a blessing. I dream of being middle-aged with a nice husband, a couple of good kids and having a double chin and wrinkles. Really."

"My dear, that comes soon enough to most of us, believe me," Lillian smiles. "But I have a feeling you'll be 'stuck' with great beauty all your life."

The big man moves purposefully toward Jolene, and she gets the clear signal she is edging dangerously close to challenging Preston's rule against starting a relationship in public. She reacts obediently and immediately.

"Forgive me, Lillian," Jolene whispers. "I must go. You've been very kind. Thank you for speaking to me." Jolene moves quickly toward the door, leaving Lillian standing with her mouth open before she can give voice to words Jolene doesn't dare stay to hear.

"Ruben, Jolene is scared to death of Preston. She is not his willing companion or lover or whatever she is to him. It is unmistakably clear to me he *owns* her. Even after such a brief meeting, I know in my mind and in my heart he has some hold over her. She's not with him of her own free will.

"If you talked with her, you wouldn't be able to tell much difference between her or me or Stephanie. She is a very impressive and sophisticated young woman. She undoubtedly comes from a good family."

"Lillian, I'd love to know what that hold is because we might be able to use it to our advantage. I think I'll contact Oliver Watterston, a good friend from law school, and have him hire an investigative firm to look into Jolene's family. Perhaps we can find out the source of his control over her."

"Oh, Ruben, you must be careful to protect Jolene. If Preston finds out, it's hard to tell what he would do to her."

"Don't concern yourself about that, my dear. We'll proceed carefully and discreetly. What you have told me about her has changed my entire opinion of her. Perhaps, we can find a way for her to help us and for us to get her out of her predicament."

"That would be ideal, dear. That beautiful face I saw up close yesterday has the fearful eyes of a trapped animal."

Chapter Four

Malicious Maneuvering

Ruben is far too wise to put any trust in Preston Turner, but even this Harvard-educated lawyer is ignorant of how cleverly his committee's adversary has maliciously outplanned and outmaneuvered them. Preston gloats as he plots with his lawyer, Randolph Grafton.

"When you walk into the meeting with them in a few days, Randolph, you can start by telling them I'm carrying their balls around in my jacket pocket. We won't be just negotiating from strength with that pompous bunch of nose-in-the-air elitists. Fact is, we won't be negotiating at all; we'll damned well be dictating to them. God, I'd love to be there to see their faces sink to the floor."

"Then why not go to the meeting and tell them yourself, Preston, if it would give you so much satisfaction?"

"Not just yet. Not now. The timing has to be perfect."

"And when do you think that will be?"

"When they're on their knees, hats off and in their hands, Randolph. I don't want to be with them until I can see them thoroughly defeated and humiliated!"

"Preston, as your lawyer, I must remind you that you are not dealing with a bunch of simpletons. These people did not get to be rich and powerful through stupidity. They are damned smart, and they know how to fight back."

"Look, Randolph, my proposal is just one step away from final approval by Western's board of directors. They practically salivated when I offered to give them the land for the rail line free in return for exclusive rights to all cattle sales in Wyandotte, as well as the only contracts to build the houses for their executives, and to construct a hotel containing their office headquarters. That leaves virtually nothing for Ruben and his group to put money into other than maybe a restaurant and a few shops.

"And when that day comes, Wyandotte will be my town, and they'll do my bidding if they want to be a part of it. That's when I'll meet with them because even as confined as I am to this chair, I will tower over every one of them."

"Ruben's group will make a counteroffer for sure, Preston. Even if you aren't worried about that, I am."

"What are they going to offer, huh? I own the only land that makes sense to build a line on. Any other route would be too out of the way and too expensive. The board either accepts my offer or gives the rights to another town. And neither of the two other towns being considered has as good or as short a route as mine, and even if they did, who in those towns could afford to give the land away free?

"You know I've spent years thinking it all through. My plan's foolproof."

"Hope you are right, Preston. I purely do."

***

Ruben's meeting with Randolph Grafton is cordial and professional but not very revealing. Randolph insists on knowing what the committee has to offer if its members are unwilling to meet the price of five hundred thousand dollars Preston demands for the land.

"Tell me what you have in mind, Ruben, and I'll get together with Preston and inform you and your committee members of his response."

"Then I presume he will not be attending himself?" Ruben says.

"No. I'll be speaking for him. But I'll have full authority to accept or reject your offer on Preston's behalf. The meeting will not be a waste of your time, I promise you, Ruben."

"All right, Randolph. Here's what we have to offer. Preston will be an equal voting member of our board, and he will be a full partner in our joint ownership of the stockyards, the hotels and their restaurants, the houses for the railroad executives, the bank, and any other arrangements we enter into with Great Western Railroad.

"In return for his providing the rail line free, there will be no other investment costs for Ruben. The other board members will pay for building the hotels, the houses, the stockyards, the bank, and the school. In addition, we would fund the expansion of the police and fire departments.

"That's a fair offer, Randolph. I figure our investment costs will more than equal the value of the land."

"All right, Ruben. I'll take the offer to Preston and let you know his decision when we meet Friday at the Golden Eagle Ranch."

Chapter Five

The Ultimatum

Ruben has some good news for the committee members when they meet an hour before the scheduled arrival of Preston Turner's lawyer. The announcement explains the presence of Frederick, who did not attend the group's initial meeting.

"I'll not hold you in suspense," Ruben beams. "Our good friend, Dr. Frederick Carlisle, has informed me he plans to build the hospital completely at his own expense!"

Frederick's friends spontaneously stand and applaud, their spirits lifted considerably by this unexpected turn of events. "Speech! Speech!" they shout in his direction.

Frederick stands and laughs partly from embarrassment and more than a little in amusement at seeing such a fuss being made over something he planned to do all along, just had not previously reached the proper time to let it be known.

"Thank you all for that sincere—and loud—but unnecessary gesture," Frederick grins. "If the town gets this railhead, it will definitely grow to the point that a hospital will be a necessity. I've always planned to build one, and now the timing seems perfect. I'll start on it as soon as the deal is struck.

"Because you are meeting today for further negotiations, I'll not go into the construction plans until a more appropriate time. But thank you for your support, and good luck with your business venture."

"Hold on there a minute, Freddy. Don't leave us just yet," Bram insists. "I think you ought to be a member of this committee, same as the rest of us."

The others nod in unanimous agreement.

"Well, I'm not opposed to that," Frederick allows. "I have money to invest, but I'd like to be something of a silent partner if that's acceptable. I can't devote time away from running a hospital, I'm sure you understand."

"Any way you want it is fine with us," Bram says, and the others again nod affirmatively. "We'll run the business, and you'll have a share in the profits. You can trust us to be fair. You know that."

"I do indeed, Bram. I leave everything in your capable hands."

***

Ruben and the other board members have solid confidence in their offer to Preston Turner. As Ruben told Randolph Grafton in their meeting, the offer is fair, even generous. Still, their justifiable distrust in Preston makes them anxious, despite the good feelings generated by Frederick's announcement.

Their apprehension is well-founded as Randolph's first sentence makes clear. "Miss Jamison, gentlemen, I regret to inform you Mr. Turner rejects your offer."

Randolph pauses, anticipating the barrage of curses and demands for explanations that will surely follow the momentary shock. Bram is so furious Jesse and two other men have to physically restrain him from leaping across the table and pummeling the bearer of the bad news.

"Hold on, hold on, everyone," Mr. Van Shelton demands. "Control yourselves. Let's give Mr. Grafton a chance to explain, and please remember he is Preston's representative, not his partner."

"Thank you, sir," Randolph says sincerely, barely able to resist his instinct to bolt out the door.

"Mr. Turner simply has a better deal."

"Who the hell from, and how could it possibly be better?" Bram demands.

Randolph painstakingly, detail by detail, explains what the railroad's directors are willing to give in return for Preston's deeding over the land free.

"Is Preston willing to consider a revised proposal?" Ruben inquires.

"I'm afraid not, Ruben."

"Do you know why not?" Ruben counters.

Randolph squirms nervously in his chair but says nothing. He doesn't dare lie to them, so he tries to placate them by stating, "I am not at liberty to say."

"What if we give you no choice?" Bram threatens.

"Take it easy, Bram," Ruben says calmingly. "I'm pretty sure I already know the answer, and I think some of you also do. It's because Preston wants to control the entire city and cut us out entirely, isn't it?"

Randolph turns to the group and explains why he cannot answer the question. "As a lawyer, Ruben knows I cannot violate the attorney-client privilege. But to get out of here with all my skin intact," he jokes weakly, "I will remind you the railroad will not close its deal with Preston without giving you a final hearing. But it must be done within two weeks.

"And, now with your permission, I'll take my leave."

***

Ruben rings for whiskey even though it's still early afternoon. "Figure we can use a good drink after what we've just been put through," he declares. "So, empty your glasses, my friends. We haven't totally lost our battle with Preston; I have some suggestions.

"I'm certain I have Preston figured out. I believe I know how he thinks, what he's up to, and why.

"First, I'm sure you'll agree with me that even the stupidest businessman would have accepted our offer. That's how good it was. And we all know Preston is not stupid.

"Second, even if we had sweetened the deal by additionally paying him the half million dollars for the land when our negotiations began, he still would have rejected it. He made the offer only because he knew we would not pay it.

"Again, I know you will agree with me that any businessman would be insane to pass up such a sum. That leads me to two conclusions: It's not about the money for Preston, and he truly is insane. Not the kind of insanity that poor babbling souls staring blankly at nothing are put into asylums for. Preston's is driven by bitterness and hatred.

"Consider these facts. His fortune is more than he'll ever need. That's not what motivates him. It's his hatred of us and people like us. He doesn't blame the horse that crippled him; he faults Doc and Frederick for not restoring his ability to walk.

"He tortures himself over his father's death. Everybody who knew Montgomery Turner liked and respected him, and Preston loved him above all others. Much more so than his mother and his younger siblings. We all saw how he practically banished them to Texas as soon as he took over the ranch when he was eighteen and had access to the large sum of money he settled on them. They left because his brother and sister were scared to death of him, and although his good mother loved him dearly, she had to protect her younger children. Preston has had no contact with them since he forced them out.

"He despises us because he sees in us what he could have been. We not only have the wealth he does, but we also have influence, wonderful families, friends, and the respect of the people in the community. And, perhaps most of all (and I admit I am doing a little psychoanalyzing here), we are capable of having intimate relations. Despite his flaunting the entrancingly beautiful Jolene everywhere he goes, Doc and Frederick have told me they doubt Preston has ever been able to consummate their relationship.

"Therefore, because of all these factors, Preston, in his twisted reasoning, unshakably believes he has something he must prove. And that is his manliness and his power. That's what he lives for."

"Goodness, Ruben, if that's true, it seems to me there's nothing we can do about it?" Gertrude Jamison says in surrender.

"Not so, Gertrude," Ruben counters. "I think we can take some action, although we stand almost no chance of saving the railhead for Wyandotte because Preston controls the only land that makes sense to use. What we have to do is save our town.

"Here's the way I figure. Randolph is right that the railroad board will give us one last hearing. And the only thing worse for Wyandotte than losing the railhead is for Preston to control the town. He'd turn it into his money-making machine, and to do that he'd have to operate it wide open and lawlessly. He would do that, again not so much for the money, but because it would enable him to grind his hatred right into the faces of all of our respectable citizens.

"I believe that provides us with our best argument for stopping him. I propose that all of us on this committee, along with our mayor, our sheriff, and our three ministers, travel as a group to Great Western's headquarters, tell their board in no uncertain terms what Preston would do to the community, how that would adversely affect Great Western's ability to operate in Wyandotte, and how much it would harm its reputation everywhere it serves the public.

"Finally, we'll make damned clear we have the money, the influence, and the power to put up such roadblocks against Great Western that its executives would rue the day they ever heard the name of Preston Turner."

"That makes powerful sense, Ruben," Mr. Van Shelton affirms. "I'm with you all the way. What about the rest of you?"

To a person, their answer is a loud cheer. The plan is set.

Chapter Six

Jolene Takes a Desperate Chance

Jolene struggles mightily to keep her fear and anxiety from giving Preston even so much as a hint she is telling him a dangerous lie. For it is not merely the usual disciplinary slap across her dazzling face she is risking. Nor is it just the fifty thousand dollar bonus her contract promises at the end of her five-year bondage. Her very life is at stake. If he or one of his henchmen discovers what she is up to, she will be dead before noon.

She pretends her sleepless night is the result of "female problems," a subject men know little about and are uncomfortable discussing. It's the only medical excuse that will guarantee her privacy if Preston will allow her to visit Dr. Carlisle's office without delay. Her chaperone will be with her as always, but he dare not follow her into the examination room, especially considering the nature of her visit.

"I must go right away, Preston," she says as calmly and as naturally as she can command her voice to sound. You see, I can't seem to stop the –"

"All right, all right!" he interrupts to avoid having to hear about the symptoms. Then go, but be back as soon as he's seen you."

"Of course," she responds, relieved that she has been convincing. "But because I do not have an appointment, I may have to wait a while to be seen."

"Just go. Take care of whatever and get back here."

Jolene quickly finishes dressing and arrives at the office a half hour later. She reports to the desk of Harvey Barrett, the receptionist. "I do not have an appointment, sir," she says barely above a whisper to reduce the risk of being overheard by the three other waiting patients. "But I am having 'female problems' and I urgently need to see Dr. Carlisle."

"Of course, Miss Lloyd. Please be seated, and I'll work you in as soon as I can."

To avoid conversation, Jolene and her chaperone sit as far away from the others as they can. With great discipline, Jolene forbids her feet to tap and her hands to wrestle with each other for what seems an eternity but is only a half hour or so before her name is called.

No sooner is she alone with Dr. Carlisle than Jolene loses the composure she has struggled all morning to maintain. She practically collapses in his arms.

"Dr. Carlisle, do you know who I am and my relationship with Preston Turner?" she gasps.

"Yes, Miss Lloyd, and please calm yourself. I promise I'll give you all the time you need for whatever problem you have."

"I'm not here for medical reasons, sir. That's just an excuse to see you. Please listen very, very carefully because I have little time, and I could not risk writing down anything I'm going to tell you.

"You must believe every word I say. Lillian will vouch for me, I believe. So, please, take me seriously."

"You have my word, Miss Lloyd. Please go on."

"My information is incomplete, but I overheard enough of Preston's conversation with some of his hired men last night to know that you and some of your friends, particularly those on the railhead committee, are in grave danger.

"Preston has an informant on your committee. I don't know who it is, but that person has told Preston about Ruben's plan to take the whole committee, plus some other prominent people, to the railroad headquarters and stop them from making a deal with Preston, even if it keeps Wyandotte from being the selected city.

"Preston is crazy mad, doctor. I've seen him furious many times, but never anything like this. The whole focus of his life is ruling this town and everyone in it, especially all of you who are rich and influential.

"I've never seen such hatred in any other human being. Believe me when I warn you he will stop at nothing to get his way. I believe he will kill or order killings if he thinks that's what it will take.

"Get to your friends without delay. I don't know when he plans to act, but it could be as early as today. And, please, keep my identify out of this, except to Lillian. Otherwise, I am a dead woman."

"Good Lord," Frederick whispers putting his fist to his mouth and blowing through it. "Let me assure you, I believe every word you said, and I will alert my friends immediately.

"You are a very courageous woman, and we are deeply in your debt. Please know that we will protect you in every way we can. So, if you think you are in imminent danger, you may stay with me now."

"No, no, doctor. That would tip Preston off and immediately set things in motion. No, I'll return to him, but, believe me, if I think I'm about to be killed, I'll run to you as quickly as I can.

"Now, please, give me a packet of some kind of pills or a small bottle of some medicine that I can show to Preston. He always questions me in detail when I've been away from him."

Chapter Seven

Intimidation

The remains of The Gentlemen's Club are a smoldering mess. Nothing but charred wood and the blacken remnants of brass beds, bottles, porcelain wash basins and the like.

The Contessa stands with Doc and Frederick, who arrived earlier to offer medical assistance if needed. The Contessa is shaking with rage, crying and making threats that everyone within earshot can hear.

"It was that bastard Preston Turner. I know it was. No doubt in my mind. And, I swear an oath that he's going to pay! I swear it!"

"Is there any witness who saw someone set the fire, Contessa?" Doc asks.

"No. Not that I know of," she sniffs. "But that horrible man has been trying to put me out of business since he set up two other places like mine. He's undercut me on prices and given free drinks and all the rest, but he didn't allow for the loyal clients I've established relationships with over the years.

"He couldn't beat me in business, so he's burned me out."

"What do you plan to do?" Frederick asks, mentioning nothing about Jolene's warning because he isn't sure of a connection, and he does not want the Contessa to do anything dangerous while in an irrational state. "I mean, I wouldn't want you to take the law into your own hands and end up not only losing your business but also landing in prison."

"Don't worry, Dr. Carlisle. I'm much too smart for that. I have the money to open another place, and, fortunately, no one was hurt. All the girls got out in time, and the clients were long gone when the fire was set.

"But I'm not going to let it go. He thinks he's so rich and so protected that he's unreachable. But when I get to him—and I will—that smug piece of crap will be the most surprised person in town."

"Well, Contessa," Doc offers, "there's nothing more you can do here, so come on home with me. You may stay at my place until you decide what to do."

"Thanks, Doc. That's sweet of you, especially considering the scandal that would cause. Two of my girls have a small house just outside of town. I'll bunk there for the time being.

"But it's good knowing I have two genuine friends in high places. I have a lot of friends around here—on the quiet, of course, not publicly. Preston Turner has overestimated his power in this town and badly underestimated mine. Mark my words!"

***

By eight o'clock the next morning, word spreads throughout town that Reece Davies woke up to discover his champion stud bull dead from a slashed throat, and Myron Bergerson's barn was set ablaze. Both men are members of Ruben's committee.

"It would take a fool to believe what happened to the Contessa, Reece, and Myron is a coincidence," Mr. Van Shelton tells Ruben and Bram as they meet in his office to determine how they will react.

"Freddy warned us Preston was up to no good, and even without proof, he's clearly trying to intimidate us," Ruben agrees. "He believes he can scare us into backing out of our meeting with the railroad board."

"Not by the time I get through with that little shit," Bram fumes, thinking as usual with his fists instead of his brain.

"No," Ruben reasons. "We have to be smart. You can bet Preston has anticipated every ordinary reaction most people would make, and he knows how to handle them. No, we have to outsmart him. First, we have to take every step necessary to protect ourselves individually, our family members, and our property.

"Let's send riders to the homes of each committee member and have them meet us here without delay. We'd better have them bring their spouses and children with all that is necessary for them to spend a few days with us. Safety has to be our foremost concern."

"Absolutely right, Ruben," Mr. Van Shelton agrees, and Bram nods his approval, cooling down enough to realize charging in like the cavalry could get a bunch of people killed.

"By the way," Mr. Van Shelton asks, "where is Jesse? He should have been in on this meeting."

"He rode into town early this morning to escort Stephanie home," Ruben explains. "Stephanie spent the night with the minister's wife after helping some of the other ladies prepare the church for Sunday afternoon's fund-raiser."

"Well, Jesse doesn't know what's going on," Bram worries. "I'm leaving right now to make sure they get back all right."

Chapter Eight

No Room for Compromise

Jesse knew nothing about the two fires or the killing of the bull when he left the ranch in the small wagon to pick up Stephanie. But the news is the talk of the town, and Jesse's experience as a former deputy sheriff and as a gunfighter puts him on immediate alert.

"Proof or no proof, this is the work of nobody but Preston Turner," he tells himself, going immediately to the minister's home to put Stephanie under his protection. She, too, has gotten the word, but she is surprised and starting to feel afraid seeing the steely look in her husband's eyes and his edginess.

"Jesse, this isn't like you. You hardly said two words to Preacher Joseph or Minerva. I've never seen you be so rude."

"I'm truly sorry about that, Stephanie, but we don't have time for good manners right now. I'll explain on the way home. But first, we have to stop at the general store."

"What for? What do we need there?"

"I'll explain on the way home I said, so don't question what I buy. I have my reasons. You just stick by my side while I'm doing it."

Stephanie is beyond bewildered when he purchases twelve fifty-pound sacks of flour, several blankets, a shotgun and half a dozen boxes of shells. She is even more surprised when he makes a narrow bed of blankets in the back of the wagon and stacks the flour sacks on each side.

"Ride up here with me until we get out of town," Jesse orders, and the confused Stephanie complies, judging correctly her husband isn't putting his instructions up for a vote.

"Now, lie down in the back on the blankets and stay below the top of the sacks. We're in danger, Stephanie, and I'm taking no chances with you. All that business that went on last night is the beginning of Preston's plan to scare us out of the railhead venture, and so far, he's doing a damned good job of it."

"It's really that serious?"

"Sure as hell is—pardon my language. But I'm worried."

What neither Stephanie nor anyone else knows, is that Jesse has never stopped practicing his skills with guns. He's grateful to God not to be living the life of a gunfighter, but he's still a crack shot with a rifle, using the stub of the middle finger on his crippled right hand to pull the trigger. He bought the shotgun because even Stephanie, who never touches weapons, couldn't miss using it from close range. He loads it, puts it and the shells at the bottom of the bed and pointed away from her.

"Not trying to scare you, sweetheart. But if I say so, you hold the butt of that shotgun tight against your shoulder and shoot to kill."

"You're scaring me to death," Stephanie says in a trembling voice.

"I purely hope it's for nothing. But we'd best be prepared if it's not. We have ten miles of danger to get through."

Bram, meanwhile, has cut the distance to three miles and is riding as fast as his mount can run to reach Stephanie and Jesse. So far, he has seen nothing suspicious.

Jesse is moving the wagon at the fastest speed his hard-working horse can pull and not give out before reaching the ranch. It's much too slow to suit him, but he mustn't let his concern for Stephanie's safety override his good judgment.

Fully alert and constantly checking the terrain on all sides, Jesse still fails to detect a rifle partly hidden by the lower limbs of a Ponderosa pine, but he instantly recognizes its distinctive sound as his poor horse falls dead and he and Stephanie are flung from the overturning wagon.

Bram, too, hears the shot and with his heart racing, he heads in the direction of the sound, rising over a knoll and sighting the wrecked wagon and its strewn load of supplies about a quarter of a mile away. He also sees two riders hightailing in the direction of town, but as much as he would like to go after them, he must check on his loved ones.

Jesse, his clothes torn and blood flowing from numerous cuts and scrapes, is leaning over Stephanie's body. Her eyes are closed, and she is not moving.

"Don't mind about me, Bram," Jesse yells. I'm just roughed up. But Stephanie has a broken arm and she's unconscious. Go get Doc or Freddy back here. Freddy, if possible; he can ride faster than Doc. Tell somebody at their office to get a horse and wagon out here pronto."

"God Almighty! Jesse," Bram cries out, genuinely scared for one of the few times in his life. "You keep her alive; you hear me. Don't let my sister die."

"I won't, Bram. Just get your ass going, now!"

Chapter Nine

The Showdown

Hunter McPhail has seen and heard enough. He was an onlooker at the fire that destroyed the Gentlemen's Club. He was having breakfast at the hotel when word reached town about the other fire and the brutal slaughtering of the prized bull. And now he's standing outside Dr. Carlisle's office as Stephanie's limp body is being gently lifted from the wagon and carried into the examination room.

"That puts the lid on it as far as I'm concerned; there's no way in hell the board's going to choose this place for its railhead," says McPhail, and he should know. In town the past three days posing as a pistol and rifle drummer, McPhail is one of Great Western's highest-ranking officers, sent by his company to discover, if he can, the real source of the conflict between Preston Turner and the committee headed by Ruben Van Shelton.

His instructions? First, find out how the community will react if the railroad accepts Turner's bid of free land in return for an exclusive contract. Second, determine why Turner is rejecting what appears to be such an obviously fair offer from the committee.

McPhail has bought countless drinks to loosen the tongues of everyone willing to talk in the saloons, and he has made discreet inquiries with merchants, hotel clerks, blacksmiths, and even a few people in his sole visit—as a nonparticipant, of course—to the Gentlemen's Club two nights before it burned to the ground.

His conclusion: There is overwhelming support for a railhead and Ruben's committee. Turner is disliked by most, hated by many, and feared by virtually all. The citizens of Wyandotte do not want him "owning" the town and, consequently, forcing them to do his bidding. They leave no doubt they hold Preston Turner responsible for the lawlessness of the past day and a half.

"We're in business to make money, not settle local feuds," McPhail reasons. "It would have been a sweet deal with that free land, but, even though it will cost the company a great deal more money to locate in one of the two other towns, at least we have overwhelming public support there."

Out of respect for Ruben and his open, honest dealing with Great Western, McPhail decides to ride right away to the Golden Eagle Ranch and deliver the bad news in person. Then, he plans to do the same with Preston. McPhail has no doubt his recommendation will be accepted by the railroad's board of directors.

***

Preston, unaware of either McPhail's true identify or his being en route to the Van Shelton ranch, is busy chewing out the two riders who ambushed Jesse and Stephanie.

"Do you realize what you two imbeciles have done," he screams, red in the face with anger and banging his fists on the sides of his wheelchair. "I made it perfectly—and I mean perfectly—clear only property was to be damaged.

"That would have brought nothing down on my head because we left no evidence anywhere. Now, proof or no proof, I expect to see that hothead Bram, and maybe even Jesse, come bursting into this room and take me apart limb by limb.

"You damn fools! You're probably too stupid to realize they'll be coming after you, too. So, go hide your horses and get back up here with all your guns and ammunition. I'll round up the other boys, so at least we might have them outgunned."

"Jolene!" Preston yells. "Jolene, get in here right now, and—oh, there you are. Get down to Dr. Carlisle's office and find out what's going on. You've been there as a patient, so you won't look too suspicious.

"You heard what just went on in here, I suppose?"

"It was too loud not to hear, Preston. But I still don't know what's happening."

"You don't need to, Jolene. Just get down to that office and be my eyes and ears there. Come back as soon as you know anything. I have no time to waste."

Grabbing her gloves and hat, Jolene hurries down the street, counting her lucky stars with every step she takes. "I'm sorry about Stephanie. I truly am," she whispers to herself. "But her misfortune has forced Preston to unknowingly give me safe passage away from him. Dr. Carlisle said I could come to him for protection when I felt the time was right, and this is it."

A sizable crowd is blocking access to Dr. Carlisle's office door, but Jolene manages to squeeze her way to the front by smiling at the men and repeating "excuse me, please" to the women. The door is locked, so she knocks until a very irritated Harvey Barrett opens it a crack and starts making a fuss. Jolene grabs him by the front of his shirt, presses her lips against his ear and says quietly but firmly: You know me, Mr. Barrett. I have life-or-death information for Dr. Carlisle. I promise."

Harvey pulls back slightly, reads the urgency in her expression and lets her in, slamming the door shut behind her.

"I must speak with Dr. Carlisle without delay. Please go into the examination room and tell him what I said."

Harvey returns immediately and leads her into the room where Stephanie is being watched over by Frederick, Jesse, and Bram. "I'm so sorry to intrude at a time like this, gentlemen, but, Dr. Carlisle, I must speak with you."

"Has the time come, Jolene?" Frederick asks.

"Yes."

"Then you may speak in front of all of us. Jesse, Bram," Frederick says, "Jolene, at the risk of her life, is the one who warned me of Preston's plans to move against us. We owe her. Now, what do you have to tell us, Jolene?"

"I overheard Preston screaming at the two men who caused trouble for Mr. Bodine and Stephanie. Preston said he wanted only property damaged in his attempt to get you all to back down. Now he's afraid you'll be coming after him with guns, and he is fortifying himself with his men in his office.

"But please, please find a way to deal with him without any of you getting hurt or killed. I can't live with that on my conscience. Please, I beg you."

Jesse grabs Bram's arm and demands he sit still. "She's right, Bram. No one wants to kill that son of bitch more than I do, but we have to be cautious. Let's wait for your father and Ruben to get here before we make any move."

"She's your wife, so I'll do as you say," Bram promises. "But I vow Preston's not going to get away with this, even if we don't have enough proof to legally hang the bastard."

**

By the time Stephanie's parents, Ruben, and Lillian arrive at about two o'clock, she is conscious and responding rationally to the questions from Frederick and Doc.

"Hug her gently," Doc cautions her relieved loved ones. She's suffered a nasty concussion in addition to a broken arm and three fractured ribs."

"Is she going to be all right?" Mrs. Van Shelton asks anxiously.

"If we can force her to take it easy, she should be back to her old self in just a few weeks," Frederick promises. Turning to Ruben and Mr. Van Shelton, he quietly adds: "Take a few minutes with Stephanie, and then we need to meet upstairs without much delay."

Frederick, Bram, Jesse, Ruben, and Mr. Van Shelton are joined by Hunter McPhail and Jolene. Frederick explains Jolene's presence, and Ruben introduces McPhail, who intercepted the Van Sheltons on their way to town to see about Stephanie.

Ruben briefs them on McPhail's decision to recommend the railroad board select another town for the railhead.

McPhail had met them on his way to their ranch, joined them for the trip to town, and informed Ruben and his father in detail why he has decided to recommend another town to the railroad but that he is willing to hold off briefly while this intimidation business with Preston is settled.

"Ruben, you're the legal expert here, but I believe we have enough proof to arrest and prosecute Preston for all this lawlessness of the past couple of days," Frederick concludes.

"Jolene witnessed an argument Preston had with the two men who attacked Stephanie and Jesse this morning. She can identify them, and she also hurried immediately here to warn us that Preston is fortifying himself in his office with his five heavily armed men in case we move against them.

"You also should know she risked her life earlier this week to warn me that Preston was putting us in danger."

"Let's send for Aaron Brinkley, the sheriff, and plan how to handle all this," Ruben suggests.

"I got it," Bram says. "I'll have him back here in ten minutes."

And he does, along with Deputy Sheriff Randy Springer. The officers are soon convinced that with Jolene willing to testify, they have sufficient evidence to arrest Preston.

"The question is how best to do it without having a gun battle in the middle of town," Brinkley cautions. "I think I'll try to see if Preston will talk with me first."

"That could be risky, boss," Springer warns.

"It's worth a try. If I'm not back in twenty minutes, Randy, you can deputize some men to use force."

"Let me, Jesse, and Randy back you up right now," Bram offers, itching to move against Preston.

"No, showing up in a group would almost guarantee a fight before I could get a word in. Let me try it my way."

The sheriff is back in fewer than ten minutes.

"When I got to his office, the place seemed to be deserted. Nobody answered when I yelled out for a meeting. I saw no sign of Preston's men and no horses tied up out front. So there's either nobody there, or they are laying a trap for us."

"What do you want to do next, sheriff?" Randy asks.

"I want you men to go back with me, wait while I try the front door, and see if anybody shoots. If they do, we've got a fight on our hands; if they don't, we'll search the place, and if Preston's not there, we'll go to his home."

Hank Smithson from the livery stable sees them coming and tells the sheriff that if he's looking for Turner's men, all five of them saddled their horses at the stable and rode fast out of town more than an hour ago.

"They've apparently run out on Preston," the sheriff concludes. "C'mon, men, let's search the building."

They hear no sounds, and nothing looks out of place until they enter Preston's office. They find him sitting in his wheelchair, sprawled face down on his desk, blood pooling from a wound in his head and a pistol a few inches from his hand.

Preston Turner is dead, apparently from a self-inflicted gunshot wound.

They find no suicide note and no evidence of foul play.

Chapter Ten

Brains Over Brawn

When it comes to a physical fight, Bram clearly is the Van Shelton brother you want on your side. He backs down from no one and when there is danger, his very presence makes his friends feel safer.

Ruben, on the other hand, rarely raises his voice, much less his fists. And he not only never carries a gun, he abhors them.

Consequently, Bram has always considered his brother to be "sissified," something less than a real man, and is contemptuous of the way in which Ruben approaches life in an educated, thoughtful, quiet manner.

Bram's opinion, however, is about to change as he and the others witness a brilliant strategy Ruben devises for rescuing the railhead for Wyandotte without a single fistfight or gunshot.

With McPhail's cooperation, Ruben sets a meeting for noon in three days, at which time he will explain his proposals. Ruben tells no one what he will do in the interim, but he wants to meet individually with Preston's lawyer, Randolph Grafton, as well as Jolene, McPhail, and the county prosecutor. Ruben's plan is tricky and complicated, but it won't take long to figure out if it works. It all depends on the answers he gets to questions he wants to put to these four people, and perhaps others.

***

As the appointed time arrives, Ruben is prepared to provide the results of his meetings with Grafton, Jolene, McPhail, the county prosecutor, and telegraph communications with Preston's mother. Ruben, with Grafton's assistance, also has researched pertinent sections of Nevada state law.

Present are those with whom he has talked in person, all members of his railhead committee, Sheriff Brinkley, Deputy Springer, and the Contessa.

"Thank you, my friends, for your presence and your patience in permitting me the necessary time to prepare proposals I believe will not only save the railhead for our town but also will be satisfactory to each of you individually. What I have to say is complicated and will take some time. Please listen carefully, and when I am finished I will answer any and all questions.

"First, Mr. Grafton has confirmed that Preston Turner left no will. That means if we don't intervene, there undoubtedly will be a long and expensive process through the state courts for anyone filing a claim of inheritance or any business seeking to have a debt paid. Quite understandably, officials of Great Western Railroad will not wait years to build a railhead. They'll just select one of our rival towns.

"Second, Preston's mother and his two siblings can file a claim, but a contract they signed more than fifteen years ago when Preston's father, Montgomery Turner, died would guarantee such a drawn-out battle that attorney and court fees would consume much of the estate.

"I was the attorney of record when Preston, in effect, bought off his mother and his siblings so he could get them to move out of the state and out of his life. For those of you who don't know why, I'll just simply say it was the bitterness he felt after his father's death.

"The settlement was absolutely fair as far as assets are concerned. Preston gave up one hundred fifty thousand dollars in cash, more than enough for his family to live well for the rest of their lives. In return, he kept fifty thousand dollars, the property, the buildings, and the livestock.

As most of you know, Preston was an extraordinarily skilled businessman—although his tactics were often questionable—and at the time of his death, his net worth is estimated by Mr. Grafton at more than half a million dollars.

"Given these facts, we would seem hopeless in our efforts to take legal control of the land needed for the rail line and thereby gain the railhead for Wyandotte. However, I have a plan that I have been working on since we last met, and Mr. Grafton, Mr. McPhail, and I believe it will work and work quickly.

"The key to our success lies with Jolene Lloyd, and at great personal sacrifice, she has agreed to cooperate. You need to know Miss Lloyd is a hero in more ways than one. At the risk of her own life, she secretly tipped off Dr. Carlisle about Preston's plans to intimidate all of us from entering into a contract with the railroad. The burnings, the killing of the animals, and the injuries to Stephanie and Jesse Bodine resulted from his orders, but Miss Lloyd's warning enabled us to protect our lives.

"Now let me briefly explain Miss Lloyd's relationship to Preston the past four years or so.

"Under great pressure to save her family from destitution after the death of her father, Jolene Lloyd allowed Preston and his Boston attorneys to pressure her into signing a contract that bound her to him for a five-year period. Why? Because of his handicap, he believed the only way to attract a desirable woman was to buy one. So he set out to have his agents find the most beautiful, vulnerable young woman he could coerce into a relationship.

"The contract essentially required her to cut herself off from contact with any other person and spend virtually twenty-four hours a day in his company. She was required to perform any task or deed he requested.

In return, he paid off her family's house and provided them with a generous monthly allowance.

"Miss Lloyd was to be released from the contract after five years with a bonus of fifty thousand dollars. Unfortunately for her, Preston died with ten months remaining in the contract period.

"However, if Miss Lloyd is recognized by the courts to be Preston Turner's common law wife—a union that has been legally accepted in Nevada—she can also be declared sole inheritor of Preston's estate. From our study of pertinent cases, Mr. Grafton and I believe she meets the necessary qualifications after domiciling with Mr. Turner continuously for more than four years.

"I will go to court immediately to have that done as quickly as possible, and Mr. Grafton and our prosecutor, Luther Shumacher, have agreed to lend their support. Mr. Shumacher has assured us he will raise no legal objections, and Mr. Grafton has promised to use the considerable influence of the Great Western Railroad to expedite our case through the court system.

"I explained to Miss Lloyd that our committee would then offer a fair price to her for the land needed for the rail line and certain other of Preston's properties required for the building of hotels, houses, a bank, an expanded school, and a stockyard.

"By agreeing to be declared Preston's common law wife—a prospect she considers personally repugnant—Miss Lloyd obviously would become a very wealthy woman. But it turns out she is foremost a woman of principle and generosity who is more interested in doing what she considers to be right than enriching herself. Totally on her own initiative, she will donate all the land to cinch the deal with the railroad.

"Furthermore, with one exception, she plans to give all of Preston's other assets, amounting to several hundred thousands of dollars, to his mother and siblings. Mrs. Turner informs me she is grateful for such a settlement and will not file any court action of her own.

"As for herself, Miss Lloyd asks only the fifty thousand dollars pledged to her in her contract."

At this point, Ruben loses control of his meeting. His voice is drowned out by thunderous cheers and applause, and Jolene herself is nearly crushed by the spontaneous hugs, handshakes, and hearty pats on the back.

"Please, folks," Ruben strains to be heard. "Your attention for just one more announcement. Please, please, everyone."

Finally, calm is restored, and Ruben is able to speak.

"We want Miss Lloyd and all the rest of you to know that her enormous generosity will not go unrewarded. So," Ruben says, turning to Jolene, "I know my committee members will support me one hundred percent in accepting you as an equal partner entitled to an equal share of our profits. For as long as we are in business, you and your family will have financial security."

***

For the first time in months, the people of Wyandotte and its surroundings feel the pressure on them ease and allow them to get about their everyday lives. Wyandotte will get its railhead, Furthermore, Ruben and his committee have carved out twenty-five percent ownership for small investors and have given them a representative of their choice to serve as a full voting member on the board of directors.

Those who lost property or livestock have been compensated. Stephanie is on the mend, and Jolene has rejoined her family in Boston where they have been befriended by Lillian's family and brought into their circle of influential acquaintances. The committee member who served as an informant to Preston has been run out of town in disgrace.

A period of calm appears to prevail.

For everyone, that is, except Bram Van Shelton.

Chapter Eleven

Shotgun Wedding

There is certain to be much wailing and gnashing of teeth—or at least some sobbing and cursing—when the girls from the Gentlemen's Club receive word that one of their most faithful and generous clients will visit no more when their new building is constructed.

Bram Van Shelton, who for forty-four years has all but sworn a blood oath to forever remain a bachelor, is married. Not in the traditional way to be sure, but married nevertheless. Country folks more commonly refer to such a joining as a "Shotgun Wedding."

It seems Bram has gotten his rich friend, Gertrude Jamison, owner of a big neighboring ranch, in a family way, and in the tradition of the West, Bram has done right by her. Their relationship started innocently enough when he chivalrously offered to escort her home after one of Ruben's railhead committee meetings ran overtime into darkness.

Concerned over Bram's returning alone when darkness got compounded by a rainstorm, Gertrude insisted he spend the night in the guest bedroom. Sensibly, Bram agreed. Not so sensibly, they had a few drinks to "ward off the chill" and wound up warming under the same blankets. Nature took its course, and Bram's bachelorhood fell victim to a bottle of bourbon.

The reaction of Mr. and Mrs. Van Shelton, Ruben and Lillian, and Jesse and Stephanie was uncontrollable laughter. Bram, they agreed, had gotten another long overdue comeuppance after years of unbridled promiscuity. And, besides, they all like Gertrude.

"Actually, I think they'll make a good match," Mr. Van Shelton proclaims. "She's his female equivalent. She's as tough as cowhide; she can ride a horse and brand a calf with the best of ranch hands; she's as wealthy, if not more so, than he is; and she can match him cuss word for cuss word. By golly, I completely approve of this union."

"I hope it's a girl," Stephanie giggles devilishly.

"Now, that's downright mean-spirited of you," her husband chides.

"Why, Jesse? You have something against girl babies?"

"You know I don't. But I can't for the life of me imagine Bram living in the same house with just females. But then again, that would be a sight to see, wouldn't it," he grins.

"Well, as far as I'm concerned, there's no such thing as too many grandchildren," Mrs. Van Shelton states. "And, Vincent, if we can hang onto life for another couple of years, we just might become great-grandparents considering Esther is getting married next summer."

"I wholeheartedly agree, Marissa. One nice thing about being wealthy is we can afford all the offspring our children and grandchildren can produce. We have plenty of room, both in our house and in our hearts. Bring 'em on, I say!"

Twenty-one-year-old Esther is in her other grandmother's care in Boston after finishing her home schooling three years earlier. She is completing her term at an exclusive Boston finishing school that combines instruction not only in academics but also in social graces and etiquette. Her twenty-two-year-old fiancé is a recent graduate of the Massachusetts Institute of Technology, and they will reside in New England.

Their wedding date is set to coincide with the graduation of her brother, Jonathan, from Harvard law school. Following in Ruben's footsteps, Jonathan plans to return to Wyandotte to help run the business side of the ranch and eventually take over when his father retires. At twenty-three, he has several girlfriends but no immediate plans for marriage.

Unlike their cousins, Stephanie and Jesse's two children are not of marrying age. After producing no children following several years of marriage, they adopted a boy and a girl, fraternal twins born in Chicago and only a month old when the Bodines brought them into their family.

They chose adoption after consulting specialists in San Francisco. Doctors found nothing wrong with Stephanie's reproductive system but concluded Jesse was sterile, the result of contracting mumps at the late age of twenty and suffering severe inflammation of the testes.

Devastated by the doctors' findings, Jesse offered Stephanie a divorce, but her love for him far outweighed her desire to experience pregnancy and the birth of a natural child. Now they have their adored twelve-year-old Gerald Vincent and Caroline Marissa.

As for Bram, he's still somewhat dazed, living with Gertrude in her house about five miles away. They plan to combine her cattle and horses with the Van Shelton's, Bram running both ranges with the help of two foremen and with Ruben and Mr. Van Shelton handling the business end in consultation with Gertrude. Combined, the two families will have the biggest spread in northwestern Nevada.

The veteran ranch hands Bram preferred living with all those years instead of residing in the family mansion have gleefully switched from calling him "Boss" to referring to him as "Papa"—but only from a safe distance.

"Now, if we could find the right woman for Frederick, we'd have just about everybody married off," Stephanie says schemingly. Lillian and Mrs. Van Shelton eagerly chime in with their agreement.

"Hate to take the shine off your well-intentioned conspiracy, ladies," Mr. Van Shelton interjects, "but I've got news for you: Freddy is forty-six years old, and after being turned down by the two women he would have married, I'm afraid he's more than a little frostbit. Besides, what woman around here would be suitable for him?"

"What do you mean by that, Vincent?" his wife asks, miffed at his so casually dismissing the entire female population of Wyandotte and its environs. "Just what's wrong with our local women?"

"For our local men, nothing, my dear. For Freddy, more than he could make a good marriage out of. He's exceptionally well educated, sophisticated, and interested in so many topics even our smartest women know nothing about because their education is so limited. A husband and wife have to have many things in common to talk about.

"No, I just don't see any possibilities, do you?"

The three women look at one another blankly. No matter what slant they put on it, Mr. Van Shelton appears to have the better argument.

"But it's such a waste," Lillian laments. "He'd make a wonderful husband and father, and time is running out for him if he wants to have children before he's old enough to be their grandfather. Besides, even as busy as he is, he still must be terribly lonely at times."

"Not as lonely as you might think," Ruben breaks in for the first time. "I detest gossip, but it's no secret that for years he's had a private relationship with Marybeth Stover, the widow whose husband made his fortune in one of Virginia City's silver mines. I don't believe he's quite as lonely as you make him out to be, Lillian."

"I don't care," Stephanie pouts. "That's awfully shallow compared with married life," she says adamantly, putting her arm around Jesse's waist and patting him lovingly.

"Don't you agree, darling?" she says with obvious prompting.

"Huh? Oh! Oh, certainly, my dear," Jesse wisely agrees, hoping that's all the contribution he'll be expected to make to this conversation.

"Still a shame," Mrs. Van Shelton maintains, standing in solidarity with the two other women and getting in the last word.

"Did I hear the call to dinner," Mr. Van Shelton feigns, holding his palm behind his ear and giving the men a reason to retreat to the dining room.

Chapter Twelve

Doc Haggerty Hospital

"Dammit, Frederick, you're not going to put my name on that hospital."

"Oh, yes, I am Doc, and there's nothing you can do about it."

"What do you mean? Am I not a grown man, free to make my own decisions and choices about my own life?"

"Nope. Not in this case, Doc. You know you can't refuse because you want this hospital more than anyone else. You can't deny that. So I can blackmail you into letting me name it in your honor by threatening not to build it otherwise."

"You wouldn't do that, Frederick."

"Wanna bet?"

"Why not put your name on it? It's your money that's paying for it. Or why not name it after your parents if you're all that modest yourself?"

"I have that covered, my friend. I plan to name the men's wing after my father and the women's after my mother. After all, I'm using the money from the sale of their historic house to pay for the hospital. So the Haggerty and the Carlisle names will be associated with the hospital for as long as it lasts. Can't fuss about that, can you, Doc?"

"OK, let's say for the sake of argument I give in with certain nonnegotiable conditions for as long as I'm alive. For one, you don't chisel my name in big letters across the front of the building. Just a modest sign—without my first and middle names. You know how much I despise both of them. No painting of me hanging in the entrance hall or anywhere else. No plaque. No nothing.

"Those are my conditions. After I die you can put up a gaudy marble statue twenty feet high with a laurel wreath in gold over my ears and lots of pretentious Latin words that nobody can understand. But while I'm still kicking, only a small sign. Agreed?"

"Agreed, Doc. But I'm going to put a drawing of that gaudy statue right beside you in your coffin just to spite you."

"You have a mean streak; you know that, Frederick?"

"Well, you're my role model, Doc."

"Sarcasm aside, that's leaves just one thing to be done with all this honoring business, Frederick. Who're you going to name the childen's wing after?"

"Montgomery Turner," Frederick says matter of factly.

"The hell you say!" Doc responds in genuine surprise. "He was a good man, no denying that. But why him, considering Preston pretty much disgraced that name around here?"

"Jolene asked me to, and she and Preston's mother are putting up the money to build the wing. I was just as shocked as you at the suggestion. But despite Preston's letting his hate control his life, as well as his ill treatment of her, Jolene came to understand how much he adored his father and always wanted to do something big to honor him in this town. She thinks associating Mr. Turner's name with children not only would be appropriate but also will be acceptable to the people of Wyandotte.

"She wants a simple plaque that reads:

**Dedicated to the memory of
MONTGOMERY TURNER
who loved his children
so much he gave his
life to save his son's.**

"What do you think, Doc?"

"I like it. While Montgomery was alive, the Turner name commanded a lot of respect around here."

"And the plaque will be stating the truth, Doc. Montgomery loved his family, and he did give his life saving Preston's. At least for more than fifteen years before Preston finished the job with his second attempt."

"Maybe so, maybe not, Frederick."

"What do you mean, Doc? What are you implying?"

"I haven't said anything about this because if I make my suspicions public, I don't know who I might be implicating. Could be Bram, could be Jesse, could be the Contessa. Or it could be any number of other people who hated Preston, including one or more of his own men"

"Where is all this coming from, Doc?"

"Frederick, I inspected the head wound after the body was taken to the undertaker's preparation room."

"And?" Frederick prompts.

"Preston was shot through his right temple."

"So?"

"Preston was left-handed."

Part 4

Eight Years Later

The Transformation of the Bitter to the Sweet

Life, Frederick has come to accept, is indeed divided by time into zones whose parts are not so much linked as they are distinct.

Chapter One

Epiphany

For Frederick, the setting is surreal. There's just no other word for it.

The room is familiar. He spent much time in it when he attended Harvard more than thirty years ago.

The students look about the same. All young. All male. All white.

The alumnus they've come to listen to appears to be like all the others Frederick and his classmates heard during their years of medical study: distinguished, authoritative, and, by their imperceptive reckoning, old.

Nothing out of the ordinary except Frederick feels somehow removed, transported back to a different lifetime, one completely separated from that in which he now lives as a fifty-four-year-old.

He sees himself as at least two different persons. One well remembers the campus, the buildings, the routine of college life, the hopes and expectations of the young. The other has learned from decades of experience the transformational effects that unanticipated challenges, opportunities, and uncontrollable events have on a person's future.

Life, he has come to accept, is indeed divided by time into zones whose parts are not so much linked as they are distinct.

The sound of applause interrupts his reverie as the dean of the medical school introduces the speaker: Dr. Frederick Albert Carlisle, an expert in rural medicine and author of numerous journal articles drawing much needed attention to that often neglected field of study.

In the letter sent months ago informing Frederick of his selection as the honored recipient of the annual Stephenson Lectureship, the dean also asked him to make a brief, informal address to the graduating class.

Frederick expresses his appreciation "for the kind and generous introduction," and, putting just one note card on the lectern, talks informally instead of reading from a scripted speech.

"I would not presume to tell any of you where to practice medicine or what patients to serve. But with your indulgence, I would like to make some suggestions.

"Some of you graduating this year attended Harvard on scholarships and by going into debt. You do not come from wealthy families, and your need for an immediately profitable career is obvious and understandable. But most of you come from backgrounds similar to mine. Your families are wealthy, you've never had to worry about money, and you may even feel entitled to your way of life. I certainly did. And I can assure you that for the first several years after I graduated, I practiced in the wealthiest part of Boston, and my patients were almost all from my family connections.

"As I am sure you will be, I was dedicated and served my patients conscientiously. I felt quite good about myself and my work as a physician and surgeon. Then I took a four-week trip west to Nevada and came under the influence of Dr. Cornelius Valens Haggerty, better known to one and all in Wyandotte as 'Doc.' I didn't suspect it at the time, but this wise physician and gifted teacher eventually become both my mentor and my hero.

"The only material possessions he had to show for half a century as a rural doctor were a couple of suits, a horse and buggy, and a modest house. But he was one of the most highly respected and loved people in the territory. He had an office in town, but he was continually on the road, at all times of the day and night, in all kinds of weather, going to some family's home to treat the sick and injured, deliver babies, and, when need be, to tend to an ailing horse or ox or cow that was critical to the family's livelihood.

"He received very little hard cash in return for his treatments. But, for the most part, his patients were honest, hard-working folks too decent and proud to take charity. So they paid Doc any way they could. With home-canned and fresh vegetables, chickens, cured meat, and occasionally even a pig or a steer. Not to mention countless baked goods and Sunday dinner invitations, many of which he accepted.

"When I determined about three years later to give up my lucrative practice in Boston and move to Wyandotte, Doc was my inspiration. He took me under his wing, helped this funny-talking, wealthy Easterner eventually become trusted and accepted, and showed me every step needed to become a rural doctor.

"And, incidentally, the folks paid me the same way they did Doc. The only difference—and admittedly it's a big one—is Doc needed their meat, vegetables, and animals to survive. Because of my personal wealth, I did not. But I took the payment anyway because Doc made

clear to me the necessity of allowing these good people to maintain their dignity.

"So, I am suggesting to all of you, regardless of your wealth or your lack of it, to consider helping people who cannot pay you in money, or perhaps can't pay you in any way at all. Few of you, I am certain, will want a career in rural medicine. Those who do will not make much money, but you can be rich in respect and admiration the way Doc was, and I assure you, that will mean more than money and high living will on the day of your death.

Accordingly, I encourage those of you who will serve the privileged classes to consider donating one day a week, or even one day a month, to assisting physicians who dedicate their lives to patients in clinics and in hospitals established for the poor and the unfortunate.

"Any of you who would like to talk with me about rural medicine may join me in just a few minutes in Room 122 on this floor. I will be pleased to answer your questions, and, if you desire, begin a correspondence with you about an observation visit or an internship.

"That's it for the 'sermon part' of my address. Permit me now to conclude by expressing my sincerest congratulations for completing the long and difficult study required to become a part of our noble profession.

"Good luck, best wishes, and may God bless each of you, your families and other loved ones, and the faculty and staff of our beloved Harvard."

Frederick receives polite applause from the members of the graduating class, all of whom recognize him as a distinguished alumnus who has brought honor to their profession and to their school. But few of whom would consider for one second following in his footsteps. One of those who does will unwittingly, within the next half hour, forever alter the course of Frederick's life, as well as his own

Following a brief exchange of handshakes and pleasantries with the dean and the senior department heads, Frederick makes his way to Room 122 to see if anyone accepts his invitation. He doesn't expect much but is pleased to hear voices inside. Only three men are present, but the sight of the one who is by far the tallest causes Frederick's knees to buckle so hard he barely avoids falling.

Frederick turns as white as a ghost because he just walked through a door as unprepared as can be for coming face to face with an apparition who looks just as Frederick did thirty years ago when he himself was a member of the graduating class of medical students.

Only it's no phantom he sees, but a young man Frederick realizes in an instant is a son he never knew he had.

All three class members move quickly to Dr. Carlisle's aid, but he steadies himself and says, "I'm all right, men. Thank you so much, but I am fine now. Guess I shouldn't have skipped eating this morning," he says, forcing a smile.

Frederick somehow makes it through a brief session, answering questions and taking names and addresses for follow-up correspondence. He shakes each man's hand and wishes him well. He asks the tall one to remain, if he has the time.

"Yes, sir, I can stay for a while longer. What else do you want to know about my plans?"

"Nothing more, really. I have all the basic information I need for now. It's just I think I recognize your name from my family's circle of acquaintances when I lived in Boston. Endicott, did you say?"

"That's right, sir. Emerson Endicott, and my family's from Boston, too. My late father was Quincy Endicott and my mother's maiden name was Blaire."

"Would her first name happen to be Honoria?"

"Absolutely, sir," Emerson answers, his voice registering surprise. "You know her then?"

"Yes, Emerson. I do, although I haven't seen or exchanged a word with her in more than twenty years. How is your mother? Is she well?"

"Quite well, sir, I am happy to say. My father was very ill for several years, and my mother dedicated herself to caring for him. But she has adjusted well since he died a decade ago. She has her 'routine,' as she likes to describe her daily life, and she seems content."

"Emerson, I'm going to be in New England for a while longer, and I'd like to contact your mother if I may have her address from you. And because we're old friends, I'd like to surprise her. So if you don't mind playing along, please keep our talk between us for now."

"Certainly, Dr. Carlisle. I'll gladly play along. I think a visit from you would make quite a nice change in her routine."

"Son," Frederick thinks to himself, "that may be the biggest understatement you'll ever make!"

Chapter Two

Revelation

Frederick immediately cancels plans to spend a few days in Cambridge visiting old friends and hangouts he was fond of as a student. He can think of nothing else but Emerson and making the short trip to Boston as quickly as possible to reconnect with Honoria. Within an hour of leaving Harvard's campus, Frederick checks out of his hotel, hires a horse and buggy and is on his way.

"Act rationally," he cautions himself. "I'd like nothing better than just to show up at her door unannounced. But I dare not do that. It could be more of a shock than she can deal with.

"Think, man, think."

Slowing the horse to a trot, Frederick uses the time to develop a plan. Honoria must be assured he is not angry she has kept their son a secret from him all these years. "This is not the time for anger; just the opposite. Right now I'm simply too overwhelmed.

"I'll check into a hotel near her house, write a brief but carefully crafted note, and have it delivered immediately. I'll have the messenger wait for a reply . . . No, no, I cannot allow her a chance to refuse to see me. I'll have the note at her house by three o'clock and it will inform her she can expect me at five o'clock. But no matter what, she must see me. I'll not leave Boston until she does."

Frederick's choice of hotels is not the best but the closest, and in this fashionable part of the city, the accommodations more than meet his needs. He pens the note, adds the address, and with the help of the concierge, a hotel employee is soon dispatched to Honoria's house.

Frederick bathes, shaves, and changes clothes for the second time in half a day. He has enough vanity to want to look his best for the woman he almost married. Or, to be brutally truthful, the woman who rejected him. No, make that the second woman who rejected him.

When he emerges from the bathroom, the time is almost four o'clock. He notices an envelope pushed under his door. He grabs it, and hurriedly reads: "I will be expecting you at five o'clock. Honoria."

He paces nervously until it's time to leave, his mind working furiously considering what he will say and wondering, as he has all afternoon, what Honoria will look like almost a quarter of a century after their last meeting.

"Good Lord, what am I? A schoolboy?" he chides himself. "Get your priorities in proper order, man."

Less than an hour later, his first question is answered. Honoria opens the door herself, and to Frederick's delight, she looks wonderful. She has gained weight, her hair is flecked with gray, and small wrinkles are discernable at the corners of her eyes. But she is nonetheless lovely. Those beautiful hazel eyes, however, seem sad, devoid of the twinkling enthusiasm of her youth.

Their hearts race ungovernably at the sight of each other. But there is initial awkwardness. Too much time has passed, and there has been much heartache between them, especially in the period following their breakup when both were struggling to recover.

"You are looking very well, Frederick," Honoria manages with a slight smile.

"As are you, Honoria."

"Please, come in. Let's go into my sitting room where I have some refreshments waiting.

"Your note said you had a speaking engagement at Harvard," Honoria says by way of making small talk. "Is that what brought you to Boston?"

"Yes. I've been writing medical journal articles for some years now about the state of rural medicine and how it can be improved. The dean of the medical school awarded me the annual Stevenson Lectureship and invited me to discuss my articles with the faculty and to make a few remarks to the graduating class. That's how I met Emerson at the—"

At the sound of her son's name, Honoria's eyes tear, and she interrupts Frederick in mid-sentence.

"Oh, Frederick, you must truly despise me for not telling you about Emerson," she says, losing her composure. "Please allow me to explain. Not because I expect you to agree with what I did, but because I want you to understand it from my point of view. May I please ask that much of you?"

"Of course, Honoria," Frederick says tenderly. "Listen carefully to me. I do not despise you, believe me. But you must understand how these past few hours have affected me. I have a thousand questions and thoughts competing for attention in my mind, and I've had so little time to sort things out. But I want to hear everything you are willing to share with me. So, please, continue."

Relieved to know this distinguished, still quite handsome man who has dropped so unexpectedly back into her life is still extraordinarily kind, Honoria begins her story at the point of her arrival back in Boston from Wyandotte.

"On the long trip home, I took stock of my life, Frederick. I knew I had just left a man I loved more than I could any other. But at twenty-three, I needed to be married and start a family. I did not love Quincy Endicott, and I told him so. He did not love me either, but his family demanded he settle down and live an orderly life, so we entered into an arrangement.

"Money was no problem, as we were both wealthy. And we had enough in common—prominent families that had known each other for generations, a busy social life, the theater, travel, books, and things of that sort. So even if we were not in love, we were reasonably content.

"You must believe I did not suspect I was pregnant when I married Quincy. Truly I didn't. My female cycles have always been irregular, and you and I had been together only once. So I didn't doubt he was the father until Emerson was born seven and a half months after our marriage.

"By the time Emerson was three, I was convinced he was our child, yours and mine. But you knew for certain the minute you saw him today, didn't you?"

"Yes, I did, and I'm still shaken by the experience. Did Quincy know?"

"Quincy never questioned his fatherhood, and I never gave him reason to. I'm sure he was at least suspicious, but he went to his grave not knowing for certain. Apparently, that's the way he wanted it.

"Quincy and Emerson had a rather stiff, formal relationship from the time he was born. Quincy was never unkind, just indifferent. And even though he was not a demonstrably affectionate man, they got along well enough without ever being close.

"Unlike you, Quincy never outgrew his adolescence, and he associated with a group of other wealthy, privileged men who spent most of their time together, carousing, gambling, hunting, and that sort of thing. Quincy never pretended to work. He had a 'position' as a board member in his family's businesses, but he rarely disturbed the dust on his desk.

"It may surprise you that I didn't really mind his lifestyle, as long as it brought no embarrassment or scandal to me and Emerson. I found my joy in my son, having a lot of time to myself, and associating with my other married friends."

"You have no other children?" Frederick interrupts.

"No, sadly, I never conceived again. Quincy never objected to our having children; he simply didn't care one way or the other.

"Unfortunately for Quincy, his excesses caught up with him in his late thirties. He developed cirrhosis of the liver and high blood pressure. It led to a stroke that incapacitated him, and he died in a confused state of mind when he was forty-one."

"Emerson was how old then?" Frederick asks.

"Thirteen. He's twenty-three now, a little young to be graduating from medical school. But he's always been a superior student and earned his bachelor's degree when he was nineteen."

"Honoria, help me understand why you did not bring me into Emerson's life after Quincy died."

"I considered it, of course, Frederick. But I had—still have—several reasons for deciding against it. One I will admit right off was selfish. But I was more concerned about the effect it would have on Emerson. He was entering those very vulnerable teenage years, totally unprepared to either understand or to deal with the scandal that would inevitably follow the revelation that not only was Quincy not his father, but I also was pregnant before I married.

"Of course, I was also protecting my family, as well as Quincy's. The selfish part I freely admit to was that I was also protecting my own reputation and social position. That, plus I wanted to ensure Emerson grew up in New England where he had every advantage a young man from a privileged family could expect. The best schools, association with influential families who could help his future, extensive travel. Everything.

"There's no way he could have had all that living in Wyandotte. And as I said all those years ago, I wasn't going to live in Nevada and ship my children off to an Eastern boarding school and see them only for Christmas and summer vacations. I would not take anything for all those years we've shared together."

"Forgive me if this sounds unkind, Honoria, but I envy you those years. Anyway, tell me what happened with you and Emerson after Quincy died."

"We carried on as normally as we could. I gave up any consideration of marrying again or even having any long-term relationships. I centered my life on Emerson. We spent a lot of time together and became even closer than we were before Quincy died.

"Emerson has turned out well, Frederick. I don't know how much you could tell from your brief meeting with him today, but I assure you, he has all the qualities I've always admired in you. He's kind and compassionate, unselfish despite his sheltered life in which he's lacked for nothing—at least materially. His ambition and his interest in medicine must be inherited from you. He also is blessed with your height and looks.

"Let me stop for a while, Frederick. I've talked enough for now. You must have many questions."

"Yes, but they are a jumble in my mind right now, Honoria. I need time to think, to assimilate everything. I suggest we need to talk over a period of time. So, if you agree, I am going to contact my medical associates in Wyandotte and extend my stay indefinitely.

"Do you think I would be upsetting your position in the community if we were seen together at your house and in public while we work our way through all of this?"

"I don't much care about that anymore, Frederick. Emerson's grown, and he is graduating soon. Let people think what they will."

"One last question before I go, Honoria. Do you have any idea how Emerson would react if we told him the truth?"

"No, and the very thought scares me to death. On the one hand, knowing could change his life for the better, but on the other, it could devastate him, perhaps ruin him. Please promise you won't tell him without consulting with me first. I will not otherwise have any peace of mind, Frederick."

"You have my word, Honoria. I promise. May I call upon you for lunch tomorrow?"

"I'll expect you at noon."

***

Frederick not only arrives promptly at noon the next day but also the next, and the next, and the next. Luncheons, dinners, the theater, the opera, and numerous other outings follow for almost a month. With six physicians and a support staff of nurses and other employees, Frederick, for the first time in years, can afford to be away from his hospital without anyone suffering as a result.

"It's been a joy, these past few weeks, Honoria, but I cannot delay my return much longer than Emerson's graduation next weekend."

"Then perhaps it's time we had a talk with our son," she suggests. "Yes," Frederick agrees. "It is indeed time."

Chapter Three

Reconciliation

"Emerson, I asked you to have dinner with Frederick and me to tell you we have been seeing each other regularly since you gave him my address."

"I figured that out on my own, mother," Emerson says respectfully. "After all, a month has passed and Dr. Carlisle is still in Boston even though he didn't plan to stay away from his practice this long. Besides," Emerson says, breaking into the smile that always deeply affects Honoria's heart, "I have my 'spies' who have reported seeing the two of you at every restaurant and social event in the city."

"Well, as resourceful as you apparently are, my son, you do not know everything. Frederick and I, you see, once were very much in love and engaged to be married."

Looking interested but not surprised, Emerson pulls his chair closer to his mother in an attempt to elicit more details. "May I know what happened?" he asks.

"It's simply that I could not live in Wyandotte, Nevada. The drastic change in lifestye and being away from my family and everything else I loved was too much for me. So, Frederick and I said goodbye, and we had no further contact until now."

"Emerson," Frederick says, breaking into the conversation, "I never married, and I never entirely stopped loving Honoria. I've overstayed my trip East because I want to find out if there is any possibility we may have a future together.

"However—and this is a very big 'however'—I need to know if you have any objections. I perfectly understand you must come first in your mother's life. That, plus the fact I still live in Wyandotte and remain as devoted as ever to the practice and advancement of rural medicine."

"Dr. Carlisle, my mother has dedicated her life to me for all of my twenty-three years. I think it's about time I put her happiness first, don't you? So, as I know you are an honorable and highly principled man, I not only have no objections, I wish you both well in whatever conclusions you come to and whatever you decide to do.

"If things work out between you, perhaps I could also give Wyandotte a try. As you know, I expressed an interest in rural medicine when I came to Room 122 with the two other men to hear further about a potential visit to your hospital, or perhaps even an internship there.

"And, mother, Dr. Carlisle's speech about the need for doctors from wealthy families to dedicate themselves to treating patients who have no means to pay for our services hit home with me. I fit precisely into that category, the same as Dr. Carlisle."

Beaming with approval and pride, Frederick shakes Emerson's hand enthusiastically and says, "I'd be pleased to have you come at anytime for no matter how briefly or how long."

Frederick's words are followed by a long silence. Although the evening has appeared to go quite well, only Emerson is smiling. Both Frederick and Honoria are apprehensive, avoiding looking directly at each other but stealing uneasy glances, each waiting for the other, or Emerson, to lead the conversation forward.

Emerson breaks into the grin of a mischievous schoolboy, leans forward, and takes each of his apprehensive elders by the hand. "Let me put both of you at ease," he says as mildly and as reassuringly as he can. "I've known for a long time how to put two and two together.

"Four things have led me to conclude that Dr. Carlisle is my biological father. Oh, yes, don't look so shocked. I know. I indeed know.

"For one, James Hillsworth, one of the men who came to Room 122, asked me afterward if Dr. Carlisle was a relative—an uncle or a cousin perhaps—because of what he described as my uncanny resemblance to him, something I myself didn't see at first.

"Second, Dr. Carlisle almost fainted when he came into the room and saw the three of us. Mainly me, I now know.

"Third, after James's observation, I went to Dr. Carlisle's hotel to get a better look at him, and he was already gone, headed to Boston, according to the concierge. That was awfully quick after I gave him your address, mother.

"Fourth, my father—Quincy, that is—was good to me but never wanted a close relationship. And I've always been aware I do not look a bit like him in any respect.

"So, what do the two of you have to say for yourselves?" Emerson smiles, pushing his chair back to have a better look as he puts both of his parents very much on the spot.

Frederick and Honoria fumble a moment or two, each hoping the other will speak first. Finally, Honoria takes a deep breath, folds both of her hands on the table and admits, "Yes, you are right, dear." She is a little embarrassed but extraordinarily relieved the secret is out and Emerson is taking it well.

"But I did not know I was pregnant," she continues, "when I married Quincy, just after I returned from a three-month stay in Wyandotte and determined Frederick and I would not marry. As for Frederick, he did not know until the day he almost collapsed when he saw you for the first time, realizing instantly he was looking at his own son."

"You must know I have some questions," Emerson insists politely, "and I'd like those answered now to get them out of the way once and for all."

"We know you do, son, if I may call you that," Frederick replies. "It's going to take a while, so make yourself comfortable." Taking Honoria's hand in his, Frederick and Emerson's mother tell their son the complete story, even discreetly about the night he was conceived.

***

Within the next two weeks, Honoria and Frederick attend their son's graduation and join with him in a small, private ceremony in which they are married, Emerson standing in as best man, and Honoria's lifelong best friend, Rebecca Hawthorne, serving as matron of honor.

A much larger and grander wedding will take place soon after they settle in Wyandotte. Knowing how eager the Van Sheltons and the Bodines will be to do the planning and make all the arrangements, Frederick and Honoria have written ahead, telling their friends to spare no expense planning an open wedding with the entire community invited.

Their trip West in a private railroad coach will serve as their honeymoon. Emerson, as well as Honoria's brother from New York and her sister from Chicago and their families, will follow in a couple of weeks.

Frederick offers Honoria the opportunity to zigzag their way to Nevada, stopping at major cities along the way for sightseeing and shopping. She politely declines.

"We've been out almost constantly since you arrived, Frederick. I'm ready for some quiet time for us alone, so let's take the shortest route to Nevada."

"Thank you, my dear. I was hoping that's what you would want. We'll be on our way tomorrow."

***

As they travel together a quarter of a century after they first fell in love, Frederick and Honoria discover that although they feel as excited and as passionate as a young couple would, something obviously is very different. Perhaps it's the wisdom that comes with experience and age-ing.

They take little for granted anymore, realizing how blessed they are to get a second chance and grateful to God for putting them back to-gether. This time without the unrealistic expectations of youth, but with the hard-earned knowledge of what's truly meaningful in the sharing of a life together.

As the trip nears its end, the train chugs along at dusk atop the hill overlooking the brightly lit city below. Frederick turns to Honoria, places his arm lovingly around her shoulders, and as they look together out the window, he observes contentedly:

"Well, Honoria, now you can finally say you are back in Wyan-dotte."

"No, my darling," she corrects. "Now I can say I am finally home."

On Sale Now!

An American Legends Collection

MICHAEL ZIMMER
**Winner of the 2015 Wrangler Award for
Outstanding Western Novel for *The Poacher's Daughter***

For more information
visit: www.SpeakingVolumes.us

On Sale Now!

"NESBITT IS A TRUE ARTIST."
—*WESTERN AMERICAN LITERATURE*

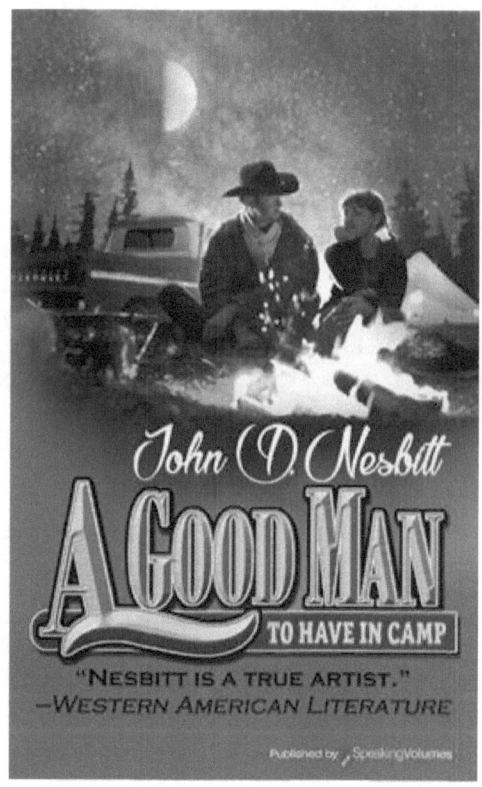

For more information
visit: www.SpeakingVolumes.us

www.ingramcontent.com/pod-product-compliance
Lightning Source LLC
Chambersburg PA
CBHW032035240626
47154CB00003B/927